He'd noticed... she'd walked into the bar.

Her hair, an unusual shade of red-gold, would make her a standout in any gathering. Did Selina Carrington's red hair reflect a passionate nature?

Her petal-perfect complexion, set off by a few stray freckles, heightened her natural, sexy allure.

And she was mouthy. Many American women were. But Selina's rosy lips were pretty enough that he preferred to silence her with a kiss.

If only she wasn't at the resort with her grandfather, Kamar's associate.

Kam liked women—many women—but he never conducted liaisons with business contacts or their families. With a sigh, he mentally classified the stunning Selina as off-limits....

* * *

Dear Reader,

From hardworking singles to loving sisters, this month's books are filled with lively, engaging heroines offering you an invitation into the world of Silhouette Romance…where fairy tales really do come true!

Arabia comes to America in the sultry, seductive *Engaged to the Sheik* (SR #1750) by Sue Swift, the fourth tale of the spellbinding IN A FAIRY TALE WORLD… miniseries. When a matchmaking princess leads a sexy sheik and a chic city girl into a fake engagement, tempers—and sparks—are sure to fly. Don't miss a moment of the magic!

All work is lots of fun when you're falling for the boss— and his adorable baby girl! Raye Morgan launches her BOARDROOM BRIDES miniseries with *The Boss, the Baby and Me* (SR #1751) in which a working girl discovers the high-powered exec she *thought* was a snake in the grass is actually the man of her dreams.

Twin sisters are supposed to help each other out. So when her glamorous business-minded sister gets cold feet, this staid schoolteacher agrees to switch places—as the bride! Will becoming *The Substitute Fiancée* (SR #1752) lead to happily ever after? Find out in this romantic tale from Rebecca Russell.

Rediscover the miracle of forgiveness in the latest book from DeAnna Talcott, *A Ring and a Rainbow* (SR #1753). As childhood sweethearts they'd promised each other forever, but that was a long time ago. Can these two adults get past their heartbreak to face the reality of a life together?

Sincerely,

Mavis C. Allen
Associate Senior Editor

Please address questions and book requests to:
Silhouette Reader Service
U.S.: 3010 Walden Ave., P.O. Box 1325, Buffalo, NY 14269
Canadian: P.O. Box 609, Fort Erie, Ont. L2A 5X3

Engaged to the Sheik

SUE SWIFT

In a
Fairy Tale
World

SILHOUETTE *Romance*®

Published by Silhouette Books

America's Publisher of Contemporary Romance

Special thanks and acknowledgment are
given to Sue Swift for her contribution to the
IN A FAIRY TALE WORLD... series.

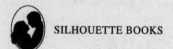 SILHOUETTE BOOKS

ISBN 0-373-19750-0

ENGAGED TO THE SHEIK

Copyright © 2005 by Harlequin Books S.A.

This edition published by arrangement with Harlequin Books S.A.

Visit Silhouette Books at www.eHarlequin.com

Printed in U.S.A.

Books by Sue Swift

Silhouette Romance

His Baby, Her Heart #1539
The Ranger & the Rescue #1574
In the Sheikh's Arms #1652
Engaged to the Sheik #1750

SUE SWIFT

Since 2000, Sue Swift has published five books and two short stories, an amazing feat for someone whose major focus in life is perfecting her slap shot.

It's fitting that the theme of her books is personal growth and transformation, since Sue has transformed from a librarian to a trial attorney to a novelist. Her books have won awards too numerous to list; her first Silhouette novel reached the finals of the prestigious RITA® Award contest. She's active in the Romance Writers of America, serving as president of her local chapter in 2001. She also lectures to authors' groups on various topics about writing.

A self-proclaimed jock, Sue is probably the only Silhouette author to own both a second-degree black belt in karate and ice hockey gear. She and her real-live hero of a husband live in Fair Oaks, California, with two retrievers and several dozen orchids.

She loves to hear from readers, especially through her Web site at sueswift.com. Her mailing address is P.O. Box 241, Citrus Heights, CA 95611-0241.

The Tale of the Robe of Feathers

[Source: F. Hadland Davis, *Myths and Legends of Japan* (London: G. G. Harrap and Company, 1913), pp. 127-129.]

Once, a fisherman sat down to enjoy the shore. There he saw, hanging from a pine, a beautiful robe of pure white feathers. No sooner had he taken the robe, then a beautiful maiden from the sea requested he return the robe to her.

The maiden proclaimed that she could not return to her celestial home without the robe, but the hard-hearted fisherman refused to be swayed. The robe was a marvel he intended to keep.

But after further pleading he relented. "I will return it to you, if you will dance for me."

The maiden agreed. "I will dance the movements that make the Palace of the Moon turn round, but I cannot dance without my feathers."

The fisherman was at first suspicious, but seeing that she was a heavenly being who would keep her promise, he trusted her.

When she had put on her garment, she danced and sang of the Palace of the Moon. Soon, she lifted into the air, white of her robe shining against the sky. She rose, playing and singing, beyond the mountains and into the ether, until she reached the glorious Palace of the Moon.

Prologue

La Torchere Resort, Florida's Gulf Coast,
Sunset, late July

As she strode through the resort gardens toward the wharf, Merry Montrose tugged her enchanted cell phone from the side pocket of her navy linen suit.

The result of a curse cast by her godmother, Merry was condemned to remain in the body of a crone unless she brought together twenty-one couples before she turned thirty.

The screen of the magic phone, when correctly charmed, enabled her to check on the nineteen unions she'd arranged over the course of the seven-year curse. She wanted to make sure all was well with "her" couples.

She flipped the phone open and tapped a button. Nothing.

"Cockles and grouse," she muttered. Unless those

nineteen couples stayed happy and married, she'd not reach her goal. She still needed to arrange two more love matches within a few weeks or she'd forever lose everything that had made her life fun.

Merry had been a princess—Princess Meredith of Silestia, an enchanted island in the Adriatic Sea. If she didn't lift the curse, she could never return to her homeland, which she dearly loved. Instead, she'd be stuck in ElderHell as an old lady with a bad temper and aching joints.

Initially stumped by her situation, Merry had talked her way into a management job at an exclusive Florida resort. A perfect hunting ground, La Torchere featured romantic gardens and beautiful beaches and attracted plenty of singles ready to fall in love. All she had to do was throw together men and women who were eager for romance.

Even better, she'd learned that some people who weren't happy were often the most willing to take the plunge into matrimony, as though marriage would solve their problems. Formerly cynical, Merry had been startled to see that love often smoothed the road through life.

Despite the occasional interference of her godmother, Lissa, who'd gotten herself a job as a concierge at La Torchere, matters were humming along perfectly.

Or so Merry hoped. With her enchanted cell phone on the fritz, she couldn't be sure. She shook the wretched thing again.

Having magical gifts wasn't all the fairy tales said it was. This cell phone, for instance, sometimes worked and sometimes it didn't. She glared in the general direction of the resort, wondering if her interfering, know-it-all godmother had hexed the phone.

"Cell phone, cell phone, let me see, all the marriages due to me." Still nothing.

Merry smacked the cell phone against her thigh, and the thing crackled to life. She shuttled through her weekly check of the magic nineteen, dreaming of when she could increase their number. Her fingers danced, tippety tapping on the buttons.

Ah. The phone's tiny screen showed her latest success, Brad and Parris Smith. They'd been a tough match, he a scruffy scientist and she a socialite too spoiled for her own good. But now Brad was feeding Parris breakfast in bed: a marmalade-laden muffin, followed by a kiss.

Hastily Merry closed the cell phone with a snap, ruminating.

She cast her eye toward the ferry dock. Sunset flamed across the sky, casting brilliant ribbons of coral and peach across a few puffy clouds.

On this, a Monday evening, she didn't expect many newcomers to La Torchere. A shame, given the glorious sunset, but most folks arrived for the weekend.

But what was this? A red Porsche roared off the ferry, driven by the impatient hand of a darkly handsome man. Following more sedately on foot came a willowy beauty whose hair reflected the reddish lights of the sunset. She was with a distinguished older fellow. Perhaps father and daughter?

Merry hurried to the front desk and pushed aside a surprised clerk. "I'll see the register now, Gordon."

"Right away, ma'am."

"And get ready to check in three guests. They are…" Merry let her voice trail off as she looked through the computerized register. "Kam Asad." An odd name, that. She frowned, but continued. "And, um, Selina and Jerome Carrington." She moved the computer's mouse and double-clicked. "All three are staying in penthouse suites, Asad in one and the Carringtons in another."

Merry retreated from the front desk to her office, again pulling out her cell phone. Pressing buttons with frantic fingers, she focused on the trio's hands. No wedding rings. Good.

Kam Asad…there was a mystery there, she guessed, but did she really care? What mattered to Merry was that the dark man in the fast car could match nicely with pretty Selina Carrington. And for Jerome, a silver fox all the way, Merry would find someone.

"You're getting good at this, my girl," she told herself. "Soon…" Sitting back in her chair with closed eyes, she lost herself in memories of her beloved Silestia.

Chapter One

Selina Carrington's hobby was breaking hearts, and she'd just spotted fresh prey.

Two stools away at a seaside bar, he was blocked from her direct view by a touchy-feely couple in the heated throes of romance. Just as well; Selina preferred to observe him covertly, watching his reflection in the mirror behind the bar's glittering shelves of bottles and glasses.

Ignoring the gentle sea breezes and the moonlit night, Selina's target held a cell phone clamped to his head. Speaking in a foreign tongue she couldn't identify, he was conducting business loudly enough to mask the soft sigh of nearby ocean waves.

A jazz combo started to set up at the other end of the bamboo-paneled room. As the guitarist tuned his instrument, Selina's prey swung around on his bar stool, a glare crossing his otherwise handsome face.

Handsome was good; in fact, handsome was essential. She never bothered with nerds. Taking them down was neither fun nor kind, but handsome, arrogant asses were legitimate victims. This one was a dead ringer for George Clooney and, without a doubt, knew it.

Selina finished her mojito and smiled. The bartender stopped polishing glasses to ask, "Another?"

"Thanks, Janis." Selina read the bartender's name from the tag pinned to the young woman's white blouse.

While Janis mashed fresh mint leaves, she asked, "Just arrived, ma'am?"

"It's Selina, and yes," she said. "What's there to do around here?" She sucked on an ice cube.

Janis sported a short rasta hairstyle, a Jamaican accent and a wide, white smile. "Anything and everything, mon. We pride ourselves on providing de complete resort experience. You can walk by de ocean or swim in it, sail on it, or even parasail above it."

"Parasailing sounds fun."

Janis's hands remained busy as she clinked ice, poured, stirred. "It is. Scary-excitin', ya know what I mean?" She winked. She put the fresh drink in front of Selina while clearing the drained glass.

The couple next to Selina left, arms around each other's waists, and Janis scooped up the two twenties that lay on the bar.

Selina sipped. The drink slid, cool and sweet, down her throat. "Mmm, this is good. The fresh mint leaves make all the dif—"

"Pardon me." A male voice broke into their conversation, distinguished by a British accent and undisguised annoyance. "But just for kicks and giggles, how about a little service over here?"

Janis's dark brows shot to the top of her forehead, disappearing beneath her jet-beaded rasta braids. Selina set down her glass and swiveled her bar stool toward the interruption.

Having finished his conversation, the Clooney clone now glowered at them down the length of the bar.

"Excuse me," Janis said to Selina. As the bartender headed toward the man, she stopped, pulled a small towel from the belt on her black pants and wiped a puddle.

He tapped impatient fingers on the bar. Selina noticed that his nails weren't merely manicured, but buffed. Her smile broadened. Not only arrogant, but her target was too wealthy, judging by the gleaming nails, expensive watch and bad attitude.

On top of all that—as if he weren't enough of a jerk—he wore a diamond stud in his left ear. How last millennium.

This was getting better and better. The Clooney clone would be a perfect diversion while she was stuck on the Gulf Coast away from her job and her life.

"What can I do for you, sir?" Janis asked the clone.

"Oh, don't give me that jibber-jabber, now that you've decided to do your job," the clone snapped.

Janis leaned on the bar and smiled at the clone. "What can I bring you, suh?" Belying her deferential tone, she turned her head and winked at Selina, who stuck her fist over her mouth to keep from laughing.

"A…martini," the clone said, as though the fate of the earth rested on his decision. "What kinds of vodka do you pour?"

Janis began to recite, "Grey Goose, Absolut, Stoli, Skyy—"

"Anything not made with potatoes, please. Wheat only. Thank you." Clone waved a condescending hand as if ordering Janis away.

Pivoting toward Selina, Janis's face contorted in a visible struggle to trap her laughter. Losing the fight, she dashed to a back room behind the bar. Selina heard a loud, snorting guffaw just as the door slapped shut.

Unfortunately for Selina's decorum, Clooney clone now zeroed in on her. "Hallo, there," he said in a low, soft voice. "You don't come here often, do you?"

He actually pronounced the *t* in often. *Gawd.* Selina bit down hard on her lower lip while thinking, Control yourself. "Uh, no," she said, affecting bland innocence. "How could you tell?"

"Oh, you're easy," he said.

Did he intend the insulting double entendre? Probably. Wondering how and when she'd cut him off at the knees, she raised her brows and openly surveyed him.

Wearing an open-necked white linen shirt with matching trousers, he looked cool and elegant even in the humid Florida night. His dark-amber skin contrasted with the linen, giving his elegance a savage undertone, as though a lion had wandered into the bar looking for a martini—wheat vodka only, nothing made with potatoes.

His blatant masculinity challenged her.

He'd be fun to take down.

"I also know that your visit here was unexpected," he continued.

"Also true." Selina gave him a come-hither look from under her lashes. "Even though you have the right accent, I didn't know your last name was Holmes."

He flashed the pearly whites at her. "You're wearing a new dress I saw in the resort boutique, so your trip must have been impromptu."

"Very good. You *are* very good...aren't you?" She adjusted the scoop neckline of her red gauze dress, remembering she'd gone braless in the sultry Florida night. Trimmed with feathers, the floaty, sexy creation was unlike anything else in her closet, and now she took full advantage of its flirty design, exposing a little more of her décolletage and dipping forward so her target could get a better look at the goods.

He responded by leaning toward her, practically diving into the front of her dress. "You arrived here on the last ferry. You bought this pretty dress, took a shower, and then came down here."

"You hit everything right." She ran her fingers through her loose, damp hair, which would normally be blown dry and bound into a French twist.

"I'm here on business, but I'll have plenty of time..." He winked at her.

She winked back. "Won't your business associates take most of your attention?"

"I can lose them with no effort." He again gestured dismissively.

"Them?" she asked.

"A real estate agent and his granddaughter. No one of importance."

As Selina's smile stretched wider, her grandfather entered the room and took the bar stool next to hers. He'd also freshened up and wore a loose polo-style shirt with khaki shorts.

"Oh, I'm glad to see you both here, already getting acquainted," Grandpa Jerry said.

"I wouldn't say we're acquainted...yet," Selina said sweetly.

Jerry patted her arm. "Sellie, I'd like you to meet Kam Asad."

A flush rose beneath the Clooney clone's swarthy skin. "You're—"

She held out a hand. "Selina Carrington." She smirked at him, enjoying his discomfiture. "So you're Kam Asad. My grandfather tells me that you're in the market for—"

"Shh!" He put a finger to his full lips. "This is high security." He scowled at Jerry. "You told her?"

Selina liked him even less, if that was possible. No one dissed her grandfather in her presence without a slash from the knife-edge of her tongue.

"So what if he did, Mr. Superspy?" she asked. "What's so high security about buying a house? I noticed you jibber-jabbering away on your cell phone a few minutes ago as if you had no secrets at all."

Kam Asad's flush deepened. "I was speaking in an Arabic dialect of my people. It is doubtful that anyone in this hemisphere understands it."

An Arabic dialect of my people. Yeah, right. Who was this dude, Rudolph Valentino? "Cell phones aren't exactly high security," Selina said. "Anyone could be listening in—"

"Let's start over." Jerry, ever the suave salesman, interceded. "Selina, this is Kamar Asad. As you know, he's in the market for some property in the D.C. area. Kam, this is my granddaughter, Selina."

Selina corralled her naturally sarcastic mouth, saying only, "Pleased to meet you." She extended her right hand.

"A pleasure for me, also." Asad shook her hand once, then dropped it as though she were Typhoid Mary.

She glanced at her grandfather, well aware that inside Jerry's mind, he was humming, "Matchmaker, matchmaker, make me a match," to the accompaniment of wedding bells.

She hoped that he wasn't too stuck on the idea of seeing her with Kam Asad. There was something of the untamed, the wild, lurking behind Kam's facade, she thought, before immediately chiding herself for her silly fantasies. Kam Asad was an ordinary man, even though he obviously thought he was a cut above the herd. But she knew better. All men were alike under the skin, whether or not that skin was handsome or ugly, old or young.

Selina didn't like handsome men. She didn't like

any men, really, and few women, but she disliked handsome men most of all.

A memory of another too-handsome man flashed through her mind, but she banished it immediately to the furthest recesses of her brain.

The only man she did like, her grandfather, now nudged her with a gentle elbow. But before Jerry could speak, Janis reappeared with Kam's martini. Sliding the glass onto a coaster on the bar, she said to Jerry, "Good evening, sir. Can I get something for you?"

"Whiskey or even a scotch," Jerome said. "What brands do you pour?"

While Jerome Carrington and the bartender chatted about fine whiskies, Kamar took a moment to reexamine the granddaughter, Selina. He'd noticed her as soon as she'd walked into the bar and had planned to meet her after finishing his conversation with his father's foreign minister.

Selina's hair, an unusual shade of red-gold, would make her a standout in any gathering, he mused, and all the more so in the dimly lit bar. Though recently washed and still damp, her gleaming hair lit the night like a torch, swinging loose along her slender neck like a silken scarf.

He was a sucker for the long, bare throats of sexy American women. His lust for them approached an obsession. Perhaps it was because the females of his country were always shrouded, but American girls, with their anytime, anyplace, anywhere approach to lovemaking attracted him like no other women. Did

Selina Carrington's red hair reflect her sexuality? He promised himself that he'd find out, and soon.

She wasn't afraid of male attention, either, judging by her attire, a feather-trimmed dress constructed of scraps and shreds of red fabric that floated and fluttered while concealing few of her body's slender curves. Her unplanned trip had also prevented her from bringing makeup, and her petal-perfect complexion, set off by a few stray freckles, heightened her natural, sexy allure.

She'd be a worthy bedmate if she hadn't come with her grandfather. Kamar liked women—many women—but he didn't believe in fouling the nest. He never conducted liaisons with business contacts or their families. The world was his playground, and he'd found many willing partners. He didn't fool around close to home.

A beautiful girl like her, there was probably a man in her life already.

And she was mouthy. Many American women were. Often a smart mouth on a woman repelled him, but Selina's rosy lips were pretty enough that he'd prefer to silence her with a kiss.

Then again, here was Jerome Carrington. So, with a sigh, Kamar mentally classified the stunning Selina and her beautiful neck as off-limits.

But he could still talk to her, couldn't he? "American women are usually such busy girls," he told her. "It was kind of you to accompany your grandfather on this trip."

She shrugged, and her low neckline dipped even further. "Grandpa Jerry thought I should get away."

"Get away? From who or what?"

"I work for an ad agency, and we just presented one of our major clients with a new campaign." Her smile was thin. "This was the first time I was responsible for the entire project."

He didn't care about her job, but girls liked it when one showed interest in their pastimes. "And what was this project about?"

"It's an advertising campaign for a cereal called Corny Crunch."

"Did you say horny crunch?" He gave her his most flirtatious smile.

"Like I haven't heard that, oh, at least twenty times before." Selina stirred her drink.

He'd try again. "What kind of, um, advertising campaign did you plan?"

"Breakdancing corn chips in cargo pants down to their ankles." She grinned at him. A real smile this time, not a fake one.

Progress, he thought. "Very charming. But why would anyone over the age of twelve buy these horny crunchies?"

Her smile broadened. "They have lots of fiber and even some oats. That'll lower your cholesterol. You ought to be thinking about that at your age."

There was such a thing as too mouthy, Kamar discovered. "At my age? For your information, I have but twenty-eight years."

"Oh, shouldn't everyone think about maintaining good health?" Selina turned to her grandfather, who ambled closer, sipping whiskey from a cut crystal tumbler. "Grandpop, what do you think of Corny Crunch?"

"A great product," he said. "Selina's ad campaign will sell millions. Another coup for the marketing goddess."

"Oh, so now you are a goddess," Kamar said. "I should have known."

She arched a perfectly plucked brow at him. "Why?"

"You have the demeanor of someone…exalted," he said. "Goddess attitude, you might say."

"Ouch." Selina clapped a hand to her face with a mock frown. "I guess I deserved that."

"You certainly did." Her grandfather glowered at her.

Kamar smiled. "Speaking of business, when shall we begin?"

"How about tomorrow morning?" Jerome Carrington asked. "We'll meet in the dining room at nine."

"Aren't there several restaurants in a resort like this one?" Selina asked.

"The barkeep will know." Jerome caught the bartender's eye. "Where's the best place for breakfast?"

"There are a number of choices, sir. There are four restaurants and two cafés at La Torchere. The poolside café can become noisy with children at play, so I would recommend The Greenhouse for breakfast."

"The Greenhouse?" Selina tilted her head to one side. "That sounds fun."

Kamar frowned. "I do not know if I want to eat my breakfast in a greenhouse."

"Why not?" Selina asked. "I'm sure they don't grow potatoes in there."

She caught the bartender's eye, and both girls laughed. *Azhib,* he thought. Wonderful. Within a few hours of his arrival, he'd convinced two women he was a fool. And he was stuck here until a deal for the property could be struck.

"Do you know what's going on here? Because I'm at sea." Jerome looked from his granddaughter's face to the bartender, and then to Kamar. "What's this about potatoes?"

"Nothing," Kamar said sourly. "The Greenhouse will be fine—9:00 a.m.?"

"I'll make a reservation," Jerome said, eyeing Kamar with an uneasy expression.

"Oh, no problem, sir." Janis removed Kamar's empty martini glass. "I'll leave a note for the concierge before I go off shift. What would the name be?"

"The Asad party." And without another word, Kamar stalked off.

"What bug's up his rear?" Jerome asked.

"Maybe a potato bug," Selina replied, and both women exploded with gales of laughter.

Chapter Two

Selina admired stability and safety, needed it, really. She worked hard to keep her life and everything in it well-organized. Her pumps, always leather and always polished to a dull glow, were neatly matched and hung two-by-two on her shoe tree in perfect order. She always bought bras with matching panties—two pairs, so one was always clean and at the ready—and folded them carefully in her lingerie drawer with their mates. Likewise, tap pants and camisoles. She bought outfits, not separates, and never ordered à la carte.

Grandpa Jerome, the only father she had and the most important person in her twenty-three-year-old life, was the opposite. Unless a maid picked up after him, his closet was total chaos. His secretary often remarked that she had a lifetime job because "Jerry doesn't know where I keep the checkbook." Indeed, his desk would remain a mountain of garbage if she didn't arrange it.

Selina didn't like the unexpected. Grandpa Jerry thrived on it.

Selina hated surprises. Grandpa Jerry liked to throw surprise parties and sweep her away on unplanned excursions. Like this one, to an exclusive resort on Florida's Gulf Coast. Less than twelve hours ago, Grandpa Jerry had shot into her cubicle at VIP Publicity, grabbed her jacket, held it open for her and said, "Come on, little Sellie. Grandpa's got a fun surprise for you."

Since Selina had sought refuge in his home at age fifteen, Grandpa Jerry had said those words many times, and she'd come to trust that his surprises would be fun. Trips to the zoo, to museums, to shops. Sometimes the museums would be in Rome or the shops in Paris.

And now, her magic pixie of a grandfather, claiming she worked too hard, had swept Selina to Florida. On the plane, he'd admitted that he was brokering a real estate deal and that Selina's presence would enliven an otherwise dull jaunt.

Selina wasn't so sure. Now, getting ready for bed in the penthouse suite atop La Torchere, she brushed her teeth with the toiletries supplied by the resort before donning their thick terry cloth robe. She left her bathroom to meet Jerry in the living room of the suite. "I don't know quite what I'm doing here," she told her grandfather.

"You're here to keep me company." Jerry lounged on the sofa in a similar robe worn over a pair of checked pajama pants. He'd already left his mark on the suite. Recent copies of the *Wall Street Journal* and the *Washington Post* littered the coffee table in front of him, and sheaves of computer printouts detailing various D.C. properties were scattered on the couch's cushions.

"Your client doesn't want me here. What's so top secret, anyway?"

Jerry hesitated. "I'm not supposed to tell you this, but he's a sheik."

"You've got to be kidding. With that accent? And don't sheiks live in desert tents with camels?"

"Not this one," Jerry said. "Kamar and his brothers were all educated in England—Cambridge, no less. His country has one of the world's most productive diamond mines. They recently opened diplomatic relations with the United States and purchased an embassy building in D.C. Now Kamar's looking for the ambassador's residence."

"I'm impressed," Selina said. "This is quite a lucrative set of deals for you."

"And it does have to be top secret." Jerome shuffled papers together into a messy stack. "If the location of the residence becomes public knowledge, the safety of the ambassador could be compromised."

"Oh, so that's why the snotty sheik was so upset with me." Selina sat on a side chair.

"You were pretty hard on him."

She huffed.

"You were mean, Sellie. I've never known you to be mean."

"You should have seen him with the bartender."

"What was the bit about the potatoes?"

"He was razzing the bartender about the vodka,"

she said. "Only wheat vodka, nothing made from potatoes. He was quite specific. Who does he think he
is, James Bond?"

"A man has the right to choose his poison. I
thought Kam was trying to be nice to you."

"He was trying to redeem himself. Unsuccessfully,
I might add. He's affected and arrogant. The man
can't love himself enough."

Jerome was silent for a second, then said, "Sometimes people who can't love themselves enough suffer
from a lack of love from others. Like you."

She swallowed against her dry mouth. "I'm loved.
You love me, right?"

"I adore you, but we both know that's not enough.
When was the last time you were involved with a
man?"

"Hey, I date all the time. You know that. You call
on Saturday night to check on me. I don't call back
until Sunday morning because—"

"Because on Saturday night you're out breaking
hearts."

Selina grinned.

"Yes, you date," Jerry continued. "But do you
ever become involved?"

She compressed her lips. "So I'm picky."

"Sellie, baby, you're beyond picky. Don't you
think it's time you got over Donald?"

She dropped her face into her hands and mumbled,
"Grandpa Jerry, I was in therapy for seven years. My
head's been shrunk so much I'm surprised you can
still see it. I've meditated. I've rolfed. I've yoga'ed.
I've sought enlightenment and personal growth every-

where I could. I honestly don't think I'll ever get over Donald. Or what Mom did." She hadn't seen her mother or her stepfather for years.

Leaving the couch, Jerry knelt by her side. "If you don't get over it, they win."

She nodded, rubbing her temples where a headache had started banging at her brain. "I know, but I—"

"Try." Her grandfather took her hand. "Try. I won't be around forever—"

"Why, where are you going?" Selina raised her head, her insides turning wintry. "Pawtucket, maybe, or Poughkeepsie?"

He wiggled her chin. "Laugh all you want, sweetheart, but I'm an old guy, and getting older every minute. You need to be with a man your own age, not some old fart with one foot in the grave and the other on a banana peel."

Selina scoffed. "You'll outlive all of us."

"No, I won't. Promise me, Sellie, that you'll make an effort."

Sobered by her grandfather's seriousness, Selina said, "Okay, I promise. Sometime. I'm still young, okay?"

He fixed her with a stern look, though his eyes twinkled. "Be nice to the sheik."

"The snotty sheik?"

He laughed. "*People* magazine calls him the sexy sheik."

"He does have a certain George Clooney appeal, if you like the type."

"Do you?"

She squirmed. Grandpop was hitting a little too

close to home. She didn't want to talk to him about the kind of men she liked. Too weird. "Maybe."

"Well, why don't you let that maybe turn into a yes? At least give that little maybe a chance."

She chuckled. "Maybe I will."

He hesitated, then asked, "Sellie, are you truly happy?"

"Sure I am. I have a great job, a great home and you." She hugged him around the shoulders. "Why should I want more?"

"There's more to life, and you know it. But for now, be nice to Prince Kamar." He winked. "Especially since I want to take quite a large wad of cash out of his wallet."

She sighed. "For you, anything...even Prince Kamar."

Chapter Three

The sharp-eyed brunette approached the concierge desk and said to the woman seated there, "Uh, can I ask for some help?"

Lilith Peterson, aka Lissa Bessart Piers, scrutinized her. That depends upon the kind of help you want, she thought. She didn't like the brunette's briefcase, her gray pinstriped pantsuit or her overly lacquered hair. Most people who came to La Torchere were on holiday and looked it, but this woman was all business.

Instead of challenging her, Lissa schooled her features into a hospitable smile, in keeping with her role. "Of course," she said. "How can I help you?" She smoothed the lapel of her jacket.

"I'm trying to find a guest," the brunette said.

"We maintain the security of all our guests. Are you a guest here, Ms....?" Lissa raised politely inquiring eyebrows.

"Yes, of course," the brunette said, a little too quickly. She offered a hand. "Marta Hunter."

Lissa touched the woman's fingers and let go. She didn't want extended contact with Marta Hunter. A strong grasp could trigger any of Lissa's array of magical abilities. She didn't want to inadvertently cast a curse or start a fire.

More than being the ordinary concierge Lilith Peterson, Lissa Bessart Piers was a member of the royal family of the enchanted realm of Silestia. Because she'd cursed her spoiled, disobedient niece seven years before, Lissa felt a responsibility to remain in Meredith's life, making sure Merry remained safe while she worked to lift the curse.

But Lissa's disguise as a concierge carried obligations, such as caring for the needs of La Torchere's guests. She said, "Good morning, Ms. Hunter. We haven't met before, have we?"

"I arrived early this morning on the first ferry of the day."

"Welcome to La Torchere. How can I help you?"

"I'm looking for the sheik, Prince Kamar ibn-Asad," Hunter said.

"Oh, I recall making a breakfast reservation for Mr. Asad's party," Lissa said. "If you move along, you should catch them in The Greenhouse."

Upon seeing it for the first time, Selina thought that The Greenhouse deserved the appellation *edifice*. A massive glass structure with fanciful Victorian-style domes and turrets, it not only housed a casually elegant café but a glorious collection of tropical greenery.

It was crowded with plants, which in her apartment remained measly little sprouts. She had a nice pothos vine at home, but here a pothos wound heart-shaped leaves the size of dinner plates high around the bole of a graceful palm, fully twenty feet into the moist, scented air. Ferns that struggled to survive in D.C. grew to prehistoric heights here.

Masses of orchids, sporting exotic colors, shapes and fragrances, were set in banks around mossy stones. A natural-looking spring flowed through The Greenhouse from a waterfall at one end to a pool at the other, surrounding a slate-floored "island" where a group of linen-draped tables were clustered.

Holding her grandfather's arm, Selina, cautious in new sandals, negotiated a rickety bridge to the island. When she'd purchased the red dress, she'd bought other clothing to last her for the week, including the denim shorts and T-shirt she now wore with the slip-pery-soled sandals.

Safely on the rough gray slate, she looked for and found Kam Asad seated at a large table. Like her grandfather, he evidently liked to read, for several newspapers were spread over the white cloth. His cell phone sat next to a silver pot. As she watched, he refilled his cup before turning a page of the paper.

A polo shirt stretched across Kam's truly admirable torso, showing muscled forearms. The emerald-green shirt set off his amber skin and thin gold watch. The only other item of jewelry he wore was his diamond stud, a rakish touch.

She couldn't check out his legs because they were under the table. But when she and her grandfather approached Kam's table, he stood until Jerry had seated her. His legs matched his arms in terms of their fitness, and she had to admit that Kam was a total stud muffin. If he weren't such a jerk, she might even be attracted to him.

"Good morning, Selina, Jerry," he said. He handed her a menu before pouring her a cup of tea.

His old-fashioned chivalry disarmed her, and she said, "Good morning, Kam," as courteously as she could, even though she didn't drink tea. She assumed that he had developed his tea habit while at Cambridge.

Opening the menu, she scanned the breakfast selections. "Too bad I don't like breakfast. There's a lot to choose from here. Even potatoes." She winked at Kam.

"You will never forget that incident with the vodka, will you?" He leaned back in his chair with an uneasy smile.

Jerry kicked her under the table, and she said, "Um, consider yourself unforgettable. It's not a bad thing."

He visibly relaxed. "Why do you not like breakfast?"

She shrugged. "It's just such a strange meal. Except for fruit, almost everything is carbohydrates or fried. It's as though you're not allowed to eat anything healthy in the morning."

"Cereals are healthy. Are there not some of your

corny crunchies on the menu?'' He waved at a passing server.

"I doubt it. At this point we're just designing the ad campaign. The cereal won't be on the market for some months."

"When I traveled to Japan, I ate soup with tea in the morning. It seemed quite healthful."

"Soup and tea? I'll have to try that sometime. But for now, I guess I'll just have a croissant and coffee." She slid the menu in the direction of the server.

"And you, sir?" the server asked Jerry.

Jerry ordered a full breakfast of bacon, eggs and toast, while Kam, like Selina, ordered a croissant. "And fresh fruit compotes for the lady and me." He smiled at her as the server left.

She smiled back at Kam. "Thanks. What did you do in Japan?"

"What I am doing here. Opened diplomatic relations, rented an embassy, found markets for our diamonds." Though he'd lowered his voice, Prince Kam had evidently accepted that Selina was Jerry's confidante.

"We have a few minutes before our orders arrive, so…" Jerry opened his briefcase and took out a stack of printouts.

"Yes, let us get to business." Kam looked toward the paperwork. "Are these from your multiple listing service?"

"Yes." Jerry slid the printouts across the table to Kam. "I weeded out the obviously unsuitable properties, but—"

Jerry broke off when Kam's gaze left their table to

focus on the bridge to the café. He said something in Arabic that sounded vaguely irritable before flipping over the printouts so no information showed. He said, "Let me handle this, all right?"

A brunette with narrow, pale features and a chin-length bob neared, whipping out a small black box from a side pocket of her gray pantsuit. Thrusting it at Kam's face, she clicked a button. The box began to whir, and Selina guessed it was a tape recorder.

"I'm talking with Prince Kamar ibn-Asad, emissary from Zohra-zbel, labeled by *People* magazine as the 'sexy sheik.' Prince Kamar, are you here in Florida to close a deal involving diamond futures on the world market?" the brunette asked.

"I beg your pardon." Kam gently moved the box away from his face, pressing the button to stop the recorder. "I am not in the habit of discussing business with women I do not know."

The brunette stuck out her hand. "Marta Hunter, from the *National Devourer* magazine."

"Ms. Hunter, I am not authorized to make a statement for your magazine. Please forgive me." Kam's voice was polite, but he barely touched the woman's hand.

"Our readers have a right to know if your country's machinations will alter the world diamond market."

Kam raised his brows. "I am not involved in any machinations, I assure you. I am only eating breakfast with my friends." His gesture encompassed Selina and Jerry.

"And you are…" Marta Hunter's avid gaze fixed on Selina.

Remembering the need for security, Selina said with a smile, "I'm just someone who's eating breakfast."

Kam grinned and gave her a thumbs-up.

"I smell a story here," Hunter said.

"I smell tea here." Although she preferred coffee, Selina picked up her cup and sipped, waiting for the reporter to leave.

The server, laden with filled plates, came to their table. "Shall I set another place?" She eyed Hunter while setting out the breakfasts, including Selina's coffee.

"No," Kam said. "This lady was just leaving. Ms. Hunter, are you a guest at this resort? I was told that only guests and employees were allowed on this island. Otherwise, I would not come here."

The server scrutinized the reporter. "If you aren't a registered guest, ma'am, I'll have to call security. They'll escort you to the ferry."

Hunter reared back defensively. "I'm a guest here, just like these folks." From another pocket, she hauled out a card key embellished with the candelabra-shaped resort logo.

Kam grimaced. "Can't you get rid of her?" he asked the server, who paled.

"You're in a difficult position," Selina said to the server, mentally chastising Kam for again mistreating staff. "Sorry."

"Just our luck," Jerry said. "Well, I guess the cat's out of the bag, Kam. We might as well come clean."

Selina stared at her grandfather. Out of the corner

of her eye, she saw Kam's brown eyes widen. The server fled.

"Yep," Jerry said. "She'll get us dead to rights."

Kam exchanged an uneasy glance with Selina, who sensed that one of her grandfather's surprises was about to be unveiled.

"Ms. Hunter, my granddaughter, Selina, and Prince Kamar have been corresponding via e-mail for some months."

Marta's eyes bugged out, and she clicked on the tape recorder. "Keep talking! Keep talking!"

"There's not much more to say." Jerry picked up his fork. "You must understand that negotiations between our families are of a very sensitive nature. We're willing to give you an exclusive if you respect our privacy until arrangements are concluded."

Selina gaped at Kam.

Kam gaped back. What on earth was the old man implying? That he, a prince of the House of Zohrazbel, courted Selina Carrington?

She was a pretty enough woman, but before heaven, she was trouble on a plate. Though he'd dreamed about her gorgeous neck last night, she was exactly the kind of female he'd never consider as a wife. He shuddered to imagine Selina and her smart mouth at a state dinner.

Truly, he didn't intend to wed at all, at least not until his royal duties required it. He knew that at some point in his life—hopefully in the distant future—his father, the king, would arrange for Kamar's marriage to a suitable girl. She would be a virgin of good family, of course, and the union would bring political advantage or riches to the House of Zohra-zbel, the royal family of the Diamond Mountain.

Selina was beautiful and smart, but she was a nobody. Not marriage material. Never.

"An exclusive? What terms?" Marta asked Jerome Carrington.

Carrington gestured expansively. "You leave us alone until after the wedding, and you get the whole story before anyone else."

The reporter's cold green eyes narrowed. "How do I know you'll keep the bargain?"

Kamar found his voice. "You don't."

"Without some assurances, no deal. As far as I'm concerned, the two of you are fair game." Marta dug into her pocket and took out a cell phone.

"That's enough." Kamar stood. "My friends, I am sorry. Let us go back to our suites and I'll make other arrangements to meet later today."

"The suites? You're in the suites?" Marta flipped the phone open and began punching buttons.

Kamar sighed. "Add the breakfast to my bill," he said to the server.

As he left The Greenhouse, escorting the Carringtons, he could hear the pesky reporter talking on the phone to her superiors.

When they got outside, he exploded. "What in The Almighty's holy name was that about?"

"Don't yell at my grandfather," Selina snapped. "He had a good reason for saying what he did. Um, you did, didn't you?"

She turned to Jerome, who put a finger to his lips. "Not here, and not now. Kamar, can you find us someplace private to talk? Not our rooms. That woman knows where we're staying."

Chapter Four

What Jerome Carrington had said to the reporter kindled Kamar's desire to corner the old man and find out what silly game he was playing.

If the story got out, Kamar would face a lot of trouble at home. His father had warned him time and again against sullying the family's reputation. When *People* magazine had named Kamar the "sexy sheik," his father threatened to relegate him to a boring desk job if he brought further dishonor on their house through his relationships with American women.

Kamar's bad temper about this morning's matter led him to rent a yacht from the resort so he and the Carringtons could find some privacy.

The rental was met with unconcealed glee by the resort manager, one Merry Montrose. Kamar couldn't fathom why. Surely none of the proceeds of the rental would make their way to Ms. Montrose's pocket. Nevertheless, she reacted to the news that he intended to take the Carringtons on a boat ride as though he'd guaranteed that his country would supply the resort's jewelry shop with free diamonds forever.

The forty-foot craft boasted a galley, sleeping accommodations for three and a crew of two: one to pilot the boat and the other to manage the passengers' food and beverage needs. After the yacht was provisioned, Kamar gave the galley crew member the afternoon off. He didn't want anyone to overhear the conversation he planned to have with Jerome. Kamar assumed that Selina would handle the galley chores while the men talked.

At twelve-thirty, Selina minced aboard, ungainly in the same ridiculous sandals she'd worn that morning. Their heels fully three inches high, the white platforms forced her to clutch her grandfather's elbow as she tottered. Jerome carried a briefcase in his other hand.

The rest of Selina's ensemble consisted of a lime-green bikini with a halter top and high-cut panties, only partially covered by a loosely crocheted white tunic that fell to the middle of her hips. The lime-green emphasized her pearlescent skin and absolutely unbelievable legs.

A white canvas beach hat flopped over her face and shoulders, protecting them from the sun. Unfortunately, the hat also concealed her sexy, swan-like neck, the sight of which was the only thing that could compensate him for an afternoon he dreaded.

Sure that the Carringtons were setting him up, Kamar gritted his teeth and swore that he would not be enticed into a liaison he didn't choose, even with bait as delectable as Selina.

As the Carringtons settled themselves into deck chairs, the pilot cast off the ropes tying the yacht to the dock. He climbed a short ladder to the flying bridge, and a few moments later the boat's engines rumbled to life. The yacht began to back out of its slip.

Selina took off her white tunic, exposing lithe curves, then reached into a carry-all and took out a tube of sunscreen. Opening the tube, she squeezed a dollop into her palms, rubbed them together and began smearing the cream onto her belly.

Kamar swallowed and looked away. On the wharf, an angular figure in a gray pantsuit rushed toward the slip while pulling a little camera from a pocket. Stopping at the end of the dock, Marta Hunter began snapping pictures.

Scowling, Kamar stationed himself between Selina and the reporter, then turned his back toward land. He might suspect the Carringtons of ulterior motives, but they were still his guests. He refused to subject them to publicity in a sleazy rag like the *National Devourer*.

"The woman won't leave us alone," he grumbled.

"You poor thing. Being known as the sexy sheik must be such a burden." With a brilliant smile, Selina joined him at the rail.

He told himself he wouldn't be affected by her proximity, her lime-green bikini or her smile. Or the knowledge that her seductive neck was now only a few inches away from his lips.

She continued, "Why don't we head below and see

if this tub has something to eat? That way the mighty Hunter can't spy on us so easily.''

''A fine idea,'' Kamar said grudgingly. He went to the galley, a space enclosed by walls at the side, but open to the stern. The front of the galley led, he knew, to a small sleeping area and a toilet.

Selina followed.

Oh, no. He'd be trapped with her in the tiny galley. He didn't want to think about the possibilities.

Her grandfather also came in, and Kamar released a relieved breath. He needed a chaperon when around Selina.

Why did the most gorgeous girls have to be so utterly wrong? And why did he have to be so susceptible to their charms?

Selina knelt at his feet and glanced up at him, her lovely neck arching. He closed his eyes and thought about his father, the honor of his family and that boring desk job.

When he looked at her again, she'd found a small, cube-shaped refrigerator tucked beneath the counter. ''Ooh, look, Grandpa Jerry. There's iced tea, bottled water, juice and wine. You want iced tea, right?'' Straightening, she poured for her grandfather, who took his glass to the deck.

Kamar smiled. Selina might be a mouthy American girl, but she knew her place: the kitchen. ''What would you like?'' he asked her.

''Um, a bottle of water, I think. The sun is very dehydrating.'' She reached into the refrigerator at the same time Kamar bent to help, and their bodies collided in the small space.

The galley's closeness intensified her scent. She smelled like sunscreen, perfume and the ocean breeze, and her slim body felt like paradise pressed against his, her skin satiny and slick. He dropped the heavy plastic bottle. It crashed onto her toes, left bare by her idiotic sandals.

She yelped, and he winced. What was it about this girl that turned him into a blithering idiot? First the potatoes, now his clumsiness with the water.

"Are you all right?" he asked.

Leaning against the counter, she wiggled her toes. The bottle rolled away. "I don't think anything's broken."

"Let me check." He knelt in the small space, telling himself he wouldn't be ensnared by Selina Carrington. She wasn't so special.

She let the counter take her weight, so he could pick up her foot to examine it. He'd never before been fascinated by a woman's toes, but hers were polished in an appealing, shiny orange that reminded him of the citrus candy that street vendors sold in Zohra-zbel.

Lime green and orange. Everything she wore made him think of eating. Devouring *her*.

There was a tiny white flower painted on Selina's biggest toenail. It was enchanting.

He kissed it.

She gasped.

Remembering himself and the situation, he stopped himself from licking up the arch to her ankle and said, "You seem all right to me," as brusquely as he could. He reached for the water bottle and stood, twisting off the cap for her. He took a bottle of juice for himself and went on deck. Before he sat, he tugged off his polo shirt and used it to mop the sweat off his forehead.

Selina stayed behind, clutching the water, then rolled the cool bottle along her cheek. No one had ever kissed her foot before, and she didn't know what to make of it. She'd heard from other women about the various forms that lovemaking took, but no one had mentioned toe kissing. She'd read about that in racier magazines, but it wasn't something that she had ever contemplated doing or having done to her.

The entire concept seemed yucky. Dirty. Gross.

But when Kam did it...a sensual heat flared through her body. She closed her eyes, reliving the moment.

He'd held her foot in his big, brown hand. Kissed it.

She'd judged him as arrogant, but did an arrogant man kiss a woman's foot?

Stop it, she told herself. *People* magazine says that Kam is one of the sexiest men in the world. He kissed your toe because it's sexy, not because he likes you, and not because he's Mr. Humility.

She went outside, where Grandpa Jerry and Kam occupied the deck chairs, talking. He'd set his cell phone on a nearby table. Selina eyed it, then dragged another chair forward and joined them, placing her untanned self in the shade of an umbrella.

"It's the perfect cover story." Grandpa Jerry leaned back into his deck chair and sipped iced tea.

"What's perfect about it?" Kam frowned, his eyebrows forming a dark bar.

"The reporter will want to chase Selina, not you

and me," Jerry said. "While we're talking, she can distract the press by pretending to choose a dress and order flowers."

"Gee, thanks, Grandpa Jerry."

"Sellie, you have nearly two weeks off. I checked with your boss." Jerry shook a finger at her. "You don't have to be back in the office until a week from next Monday. You can take an afternoon or two to look at some catalogs."

Selina scrutinized Jerry, who'd put her into an untenable position. Last night, she'd promised that she'd be nice to Prince Kamar, but at the time she hadn't known what "being nice" would entail. If she didn't cooperate, Jerry would think she was reneging. He'd guilt trip her all the way to Timbuktu and Kalamazoo.

"Okay, I'll pretend to be his girlfriend—under one condition." She pointed her water bottle at Kam. "You have to be nicer to people."

"Me? I am perfectly nice to people. Everyone loves me."

"You are not perfectly nice to people, and people don't love you. I saw you with that bartender last night."

"She was quite negligent." Kamar sipped juice.

"She was not negligent, and you were an arrogant buffoon."

"Selina!" Jerome looked scandalized.

Ignoring her grandfather, she went on. "I won't be the girlfriend or fiancée, or whatever, of an arrogant buffoon."

"You are calling a prince of the Zohra-zbel an arrogant buffoon?'' His unibrow was now punctuated by two deep furrows above his nose.

"If you're a prince of the Zohra-z-whatever, then yes, I guess I am.''

He sat back, clearly bewildered. "I am an arrogant buffoon? No other woman has told me that.''

"Maybe you never made a spectacle of yourself the way you did last night,'' Selina said, "but I doubt it.''

"Me? A spectacle? How was I a spectacle?'' He twirled the stem of his Matrix-style sunglasses.

Selina grinned. "How were you *not* a spectacle?''

"The bartender was a complete twit.'' Kam's stuffy British accent had become more pronounced.

"A twit? Did you actually call her a twit?'' Selina laughed.

"Yes. As in nitwit.''

"The bartender, whose name is Janis, by the way, politely left you alone rather than intruding so you could complete your phone call without interruption.''

"But I wanted to drink while I talked on the phone.''

"She's not psychic. How's she supposed to know that?''

"She's supposed to ask.''

"But if she asked, she'd interrupt your conversation.''

His eyes shifted. "True.''

"On top of that, why were you on your cell phone in that bar to begin with?''

He looked nonplussed.

"Do you suppose that the rest of the world wants to hear your phone call?''

He recovered. "Of course not. That is why I was speaking in the tongue of my people."

"You shouldn't have been speaking at all."

"Ah, you would have me seen but not heard."

"Now you're getting the idea." Selina smiled sweetly. "It's just simple PR."

"What is this pee-are?"

"Public relations. I hope that the ambassador from your country to the United States doesn't behave so boorishly in public."

"It so happens I have been offered the job."

"Oh, really? Did you take it?"

"No."

"Good."

"Not yet. I'm considering it."

"Well, consider this." She leaned forward. "Being an ambassador requires diplomacy."

"But of course. I will be wonderful. Like I told you, everyone loves me."

"Pfft. You have no idea."

"So you're both in agreement?" Jerome Carrington looked from his granddaughter to Kamar. "You'll play this game until the deal's concluded?"

Kamar studied Selina, attempting to divine her involvement in this fiasco. She seemed…resigned. Not surprised but resigned, as though she knew what scheme Jerome planned, accepted it, but was not particularly happy about it.

Jerome's countenance was as bland as the full moon. He opened his briefcase and removed a rubber-banded bundle of papers. Apparently taking their silence as assent, Jerry said, "Now, since that's settled, shall we?'' He snapped off the rubber bands, unrolling the tube of MLS printouts.

"Look here, nobody has asked me what I think," Kamar said.

"What's the problem?'' Jerry asked. "The seed is already planted in Marta Hunter's mind. All the two of you have to do is hang around together. She'll see what she wants to see, hear what she wants to hear."

"Hmm." Kamar knew the old man was right. People tended to believe what they wanted to believe rather than what was true. "She does seem to be thrown well off the track. Dinner tonight, then, Selina?"

Her eyes narrowed. "I guess so."

"What could be the harm?" Jerry asked.

Chapter Five

Selina didn't know why, but as soon as they docked, she embarked on a mad orgy of purchasing and primping she ascribed to FDN, Feminine Dating Neurosis. She hated FDN, but it seemed to be a permanent, incurable condition. She did the same silly things every date night: checked her closet, found nothing to wear, went shopping to buy an outfit she'd never wear again, got her hair styled and her nails manicured.

Rationalizing, she told herself that here at La Torchere she had a real reason to shop. She literally had nothing to wear. When she'd arrived, she'd bought only one dress, the red one with feathers, and she couldn't wear the same distinctive outfit two nights in a row. After she'd washed her hair, she hadn't styled it, just let it dry, flopping to her shoulders. She'd gotten away with shoving it under a hat during the day, but the casual canvas number wasn't suitable for dinner. On top of all that, she really needed a manicure. She really did.

She was pretty sure that Kam liked her pedicure, so she didn't change it.

Though she recognized her bizarre behaviors, she didn't know why she bothered. She didn't know why she *ever* bothered, but especially tonight. She didn't like Kam. She didn't like any of the men she dated, but all the same, every Saturday she went through the same routine: closet, panic, shop, hair, nails.

By the time Kam tapped on her door, she was ready, her cool façade in place with none of her internal turmoil showing. She'd picked a white satin slip dress, which showed off her throat and shoulders. The stylist had swept her hair into a soft updo, leaving curls to brush her cheek and neck. Hammered silver crescents dangled from her earlobes, and she draped a silver shawl over her bare arms. She'd bought makeup and applied it.

Like the previous night, Kam wore loose white linen. As he walked her to one of the resort's restaurants—the one by the beach—she decided that the look suited him.

When they entered the restaurant, the maître d' showed them to a table close to the kitchen's bustle. Worse, Marta Hunter was seated two tables away from theirs. A frown crossed Kam's face, and he asked, "Might we sit elsewhere?"

"Where would you prefer, sir?" the maître d' asked, his posture rigid.

"Away from the kitchen."

With Kam's tone bordering on rudeness, Selina in-

tervened. "Um, could we sit near the beach?" she
asked brightly. "I just love the ocean view from your
restaurant."

The maître d's features relaxed. "Sure, I can do
that for you, ma'am." He escorted them to a table
next to an open window that admitted the sea breezes,
and seated Selina facing west, toward the sunset.
Sinking behind a bank of clouds, the sun flung coral
and lemon ribbons across the darkening sky. The air,
though cooling, remained sultry.

He showed Kam to the chair opposite hers, which
he refused. "I'd like to sit next to my fiancée, so we
can both watch the sunset," Kam said, placing his cell
phone on the table next to his bread plate.

"Of course, sir." The maître d's voice remained
bland.

Kam leaned closer to the maître d', slipping him a
bill. "Make sure we are not interrupted," he said in
a low tone. "There is a woman seated near the
kitchen, in the gray suit, who may try to approach us
or take a photo."

The maître d' stiffened. "Not on my watch." He
shoved the bill into an inner pocket of his dinner suit,
then moved a potted ficus away from the wall so it
screened their table from the rest of the dining room.

After the maître d' left, Kam sat next to Selina,
moving his chair closer than she liked, but she wasn't
going to make an issue out of it. It was part of the
trick they had to play on the reporter, she supposed.

He'd called her his fiancée. What a joke, especially
since the evening was developing into another awful
dinner date with a bore who thought that arrogance to

the wait staff would impress a woman. Nothing could be further from the truth, as far as she was concerned. She was never rude to staff; each person she met was a potential consumer of her products.

And to make the situation worse, she was trapped. Trapped on this island, trapped by her promise to Grandpa Jerry to be nice to Prince Kamar, trapped by Jerry's crazy plan to pretend she and Kam were an item.

She was glad Marta Hunter had shown up. If not, Selina would have had to suffer through a horrible date for no reason.

She asked Kam, "How did that woman know we were here?"

"I made a reservation." He stretched out long legs beneath the table, crossing them at the ankles. "She must be getting information from the hotel staff."

A server brought water, bread and menus in a bustle of activity. Kam perused the wine list as though he researched the secret to eternal life.

With no patience for wine snobs, Selina instead watched the dusk deepen. As the sky darkened from cobalt to indigo, a silvery moon came out. Close to full, it shone through the palms fringing the shore, casting feathery shadows across the sand. Seabirds' cries, plaintive and shrill, occasionally rose above the soft sigh of the waves breaking against the beach.

"Would you prefer burgundy or Pouilly-Fumé?" Kam asked her.

"I don't know. Maybe we should order first, or ask the wine steward."

"I do not need to ask a hired hand what to order."

Selina raised her brows. "The sommelier's an expert."

"So am I."

The sommelier arrived to take their wine order. Kam opened his mouth to speak, but Selina nudged his leg with her shoe. "Let me," she said.

In a big show of pain, Kam rubbed his calf while she sweet-talked the sommelier, trying to resurrect the good will of the restaurant staff. Otherwise, she and Kam could be victimized by bad service the entire evening.

She smiled at the wine steward. "Would you recommend the burgundy or the Pouilly-Fumé?"

His chest puffed out a tad. "That depends upon your dinner order. Should you order the lobster—and I would highly recommend it—I'd steer you toward the Pouilly-Fumé. But, I happen to know that a fresh shipment of lamb arrived today, which is our chef's specialty. A red burgundy would be my choice with the lamb."

"Oh." Selina fluttered her lashes. "May I ask how long you've been a connoisseur of fine vintages?"

The man preened. "Twelve years, ma'am." He glanced at Kamar, who scowled. The sommelier backed away, saying, "Um, shall I give you two a moment to decide?"

"I'll bet you anything that he'll return with wine samples from what's open at the bar—if you didn't scare him off with that frown." Selina compressed her lips, settling back into her chair. Her thigh pressed against his.

He felt warm and wonderful, so she quickly edged

away. She might have to pretend to like him, but she wasn't going to get involved. Touching him was a bad idea. And there would be no more toe kissing.

Kam's glower deepened. "A prince of the Zohra-zbel does not need to manipulate a wine server."

The next two weeks would be purgatory if Kam kept up the prince act. "I'm not being manipulative, I'm being nice. I'm acknowledging the man's exper-tise and allowing him to feel good about himself."

"You smile at him, but there is no joy or sincerity within you. It is but a sham, a game you play to toy with others."

Selina's mind blanked. Trying to collect her thoughts and respond, she looked at their table, noting the immaculate white cloth, the moonlight glittering on cut crystal and fine silver.

Kam continued, "You believe that I am arrogant. I merely ask for what I want."

She found her tongue. "You don't ask, you order."

"I am honest and straightforward." He put one fin-ger on her chin and turned her head, forcing her to see him. His dark eyes shone with intelligence. "When we met, you flirted with me as though you liked me. You had already decided what you felt, but you were not honest. I was just something to play with, a toy."

"Sauce for the goose." She tilted her chin away from his hand but continued to watch him. His insight had surprised her, and she wanted to understand that, and him, without revealing anything of herself. He had already figured out too much, and she didn't want to give herself away. If she gave too much, she might have nothing left.

He dropped his hand, covering hers, which lay on the table.

She didn't move, knowing that to show fear to a predator was fatal. She said, "I can't help but guess that a man known as the 'sexy sheik' toys with women." Despite herself, her hand trembled beneath his.

"That may be true."

Score one for me, she thought. "So?"

"So perhaps we both play the same game. Why do you play this game, Selina?" His hand pressed down on hers, his palm warm and possessive.

To distance herself, she looked away, toward the waves sliding up the sand. "To amuse myself."

"Oh, I do not think you are truly amused." He played with her hand, tapping each of her newly painted nails, starting from the pinky and going toward her thumb. His touch burned. "You are beautiful, yes, but so unhappy."

She cut him a hard stare. "Says who?"

"I say so."

"Therefore it must be true." She managed to keep her tone light, despite her rising fury. No matter what he said, she wouldn't cause a scene. To the reporter, or anyone else who might be watching, they must have looked like a happy couple: he caressing her hand, she smiling. No one else could know that he growled his words while her mouth was open in a snarl.

"I believe it is true. Do you deny it, Selina?" He

leaned toward her, his warmth enveloping. "I play games with women, yes, but I have fun. And I can truly say that no woman has left my bed unhappy. But you, you play games but are not happy. What, then, is the purpose?"

The sommelier returned, a server in tow. Kamar said, "No wine tonight, I think." He glanced at Selina. "What would you like to eat?"

She didn't dispute his refusal of wine. Allowing alcohol to loosen her up around Kamar would be stupid. He'd shown unexpected depth, and she wanted to be clear-headed when dealing with him. "The lobster, please," she said through tight lips.

"Two lobster dinners, salad and so forth," Kamar said to the server.

"Certainly, sir."

"Try, at least, to look happy." Kam continued to play with her fingers. "The mighty Hunter, as you have called her, is approaching."

"Great," Selina said, just before he used one big hand to turn her head toward his for a kiss.

He started out slowly, sliding his full, seductive mouth over hers before nibbling on her lower lip as though asking for admittance. Not to be outdone, she opened to him, and he slipped his tongue inside, searching for hers. She met him halfway, darting only the sharp tip of her tongue against his, then withdrawing, challenging him to follow and chase.

His hand clenched in her hair, and he tugged her head back, leaving her mouth, trailing open, wet kisses along her throat.

She hadn't expected such a blatant public display,

but she wouldn't be the first to show the white feather. He returned to her lips with a full-on soul kiss that spun her mind into space and her body into heaven.

A rustle told her that a server had arrived. She blinked, pulling away from Kam's embrace, but he didn't let her go far. Keeping a possessive arm around her bare shoulders, he fingered her neck while the server put salads in front of them. Another set a votive candle in a crystal holder on their table; while they'd kissed, full night had fallen.

Selina pulled herself together, realizing *People* magazine hadn't lied. In addition to his blatant good looks, Prince Kamar's kiss packed one heck of a wallop. Jerry's plan had definite merits, as long as it didn't go too far. Kissing was okay, but anything more wasn't on her schedule.

With his fork, Kam stabbed a lettuce leaf. After swirling it in the dressing, he guided the fork to her lips.

"Why?" she asked.

"It's your goddess attitude," he said. "Divinities exist to be served, do they not?"

She hesitated, wondering if he mocked her, then decided it didn't matter. She let him feed her the bite of salad. With deliberation she chewed and swallowed, immersed in his gaze, which held her even more tightly than his embrace. Dark and mysterious as the midnight sea, his eyes captivated her. What lay behind those seductive pools?

She reached for her water glass while he ate. He'd gotten to her so completely that she had to clutch the goblet to avoid dropping it.

She breathed, once, twice, three times, very deeply, the way she'd learned in yoga class.

He kissed, offered her food, ate, then kissed her again and again between bites, each kiss intimate, searching, knowing.

What was her yoga meditation mantra? Why had she forgotten it when she really needed it?

She'd forgotten everything, really, except the satisfaction of taking the pleasure offered by this beautiful man. Maybe her nagging about his arrogance had gotten to him, because he'd become as attentive as a bridegroom on his wedding night.

"Don't look around," he murmured into her ear as the server took away their salad plates. "But the mighty Hunter again draws nigh."

She forced a smile. So this was why he was being so charming: Hunter. Selina had forgotten, forgotten their true situation amid the sweet kisses on her mouth and the richer caresses of his full lips along her throat.

Their dinners appeared. The meal was excellent, and Kam's approach to eating it, blindingly sensual. Selina fought to maintain emotional distance while enjoying Kam, taunting him with her mouth, her eyes, knowing he'd never have her. Her body softened and heated, but she told herself over and over that it didn't mean anything. She meant nothing to Kam, and, despite the growing desire raising her temperature to a fever pitch, he meant nothing to her. He was this week's companion and her partner in trickery. That was all.

By the time they'd finished their meal, the restaurant had emptied. Even Hunter had given up on getting any information and left.

Kam signed the bill and stood, holding out a hand to Selina. "Shall we?"

Chapter Six

Selina stared at Kam, her mind in a fog, her body tortured by a heated desire she'd never before felt. "Shall we...what?" He didn't want to go to bed with her, did he? She hardly knew him. She'd told Jerry she'd be nice to the sheik, but she wasn't going to give it up to Prince Kamar and knew that her grandfather didn't expect that of her. She wasn't interested in becoming another notation in the world-famous sexy sheik's day planner. Not now, not ever.

"Leave. It is quite late, my goddess."

"You're right. The staff probably wants to clean up and go home." She managed a chuckle, but it was tough. She'd never before lost track of time because of a man's kisses.

"Will you walk with me on the beach before retiring?"

She could handle a walk, couldn't she? "Sh-sure." Rising, she arranged her shawl over her elbows.

He draped an arm along her bare shoulders to lead her out, and she couldn't suppress a shiver.

"Cold?" he asked, drawing her closer.

"I'm okay." She couldn't tell Kam what that shiver meant, because it was a shiver of longing. She had to cover that shiver up, bury that longing deep, maintain at least a shred of control. She would not be defeated by a shiver or by an arrogant foreign princeling who didn't know who she was or what she'd been through.

He got to her in a way no other man had ever managed—and plenty had tried. She hated that. She didn't want anyone to get to her, ever.

Worse, he'd looked beyond the games she'd played to see her deep-seated misery. She hated that even more. Her feelings weren't Kam's business, and she was sure he didn't really care. After all, they played the same game, didn't they? The game of not caring, pretending involvement yet remaining apart, having fun without true intimacy or commitment.

She was sure of something else: Sheik Kamar didn't play for the same reasons she did. He was easy to figure out, the spoiled scion of a culture that didn't respect women, he saw females as playthings. She doubted that he was any more complex than the other Peter Pans she'd dated.

With an effort, she dismissed him as a person while accepting his arm guiding her toward the ocean.

Outside the restaurant a lawn sloped down to the water's edge, dotted by clumps of hibiscus and ginger, their flowers lustrous in the moonlight. The scents of tropical foliage mingled with the aromas of sea, sand

and Kam, who wore a spicy fragrance that reminded her of mysterious ports of call and exotic bazaars.

The moon, high in the ebony sky, told her that midnight approached. Though cooler than during the day, the sultry air brushed her skin with a gentle caress.

When they reached the boundary between grass and sand, Selina stopped to kick off her shoes. She didn't own anything else like the white platform heels, and she didn't want to ruin them on the beach.

"Selina, look." Kam, who'd walked to the shoreline, pointed. "What is this?"

She looked, then gasped with delight. The waves were edged with a glow like fireflies on a summer night. "I don't know." She bent, careful to keep her hem dry and scooped up a little water. Phosphorescent liquid streamed from her fingers.

"Look at it." Kam sounded awed. The entire long beach was lined with the eerie luminescence.

"What is it?"

"I don't know, but it's amazing." They turned to walk along the shoreline, with the sea to their left, the resort and its facilities to their right. The strand stretched out before them, shining in the moonlight, an enchanted highway beneath the stars, bordered by the magic shimmering waves. At the far, curved end of the beach, darkness reigned; a mangrove forest, she supposed. Her feet sank in the sand as they walked, and she leaned on Kam's arm for support.

They passed villas, detached little houses where couples or families could find even greater privacy than the resort hotel, surrounded by elaborately designed gardens. Swimming pools gleamed aquamarine, with waterfalls and natural rock decor adding to their allure.

Farther on, they approached the bar where they'd met the night before. Kam must have noticed, too, because he said, "Look here," and pointed. Through the unglassed window, Selina saw Janis and Marta Hunter talking, though she couldn't hear anything over the music from the band, which was winding up "It Had To Be You."

"I hope that twit of a bartender doesn't gossip about us to the reporter," Kam grumbled.

"She's not a twit, and I think we can rely on Janis's discretion."

"She didn't like me much."

Selina opened her eyes very wide. "Didn't you say earlier that everyone loves you?"

"Not everyone," he said with emphasis.

She grinned, pleased to have poked a hole in his massive self-regard.

The band started "Unforgettable," and he turned his head to smile at her. "Should this be our song?"

"Our song? Why should we have a song?"

"We're a couple, at least for now. Don't couples have a special song?"

"Some do. Why this one?"

He shrugged. "You told me this morning that I'm unforgettable."

Remembering, she giggled. "Oh, yeah."

"I could easily feel the same way about you." He took her into his arms and began to dance, following the slow and easy beat. She didn't dance often, but

Kam made it effortless, sweeping her along with the music, the sea and the sky.

She felt the boundaries between them start to dissolve, her carefully honed and sharpened edges heating, softening, expanding to include Kam. She murmured, "We're making a spectacle of ourselves."

His smile was lazy, sensual, sexy. "I thought that was the idea." He pressed his hips to hers, his desire too blatant for her restrained taste. Had the man no subtlety?

She eased her body away a couple of inches. "No sense in going overboard, is there? I'm not interested in becoming another fleeting overnight memory of yours." She strove to keep her tone light, casual.

"Why not? It's fun. Besides, I bet you've had lots of boyfriends, a beautiful young woman like you."

She lifted her chin. "You'd lose that bet."

He stopped dancing to stare at her. "You are the most surprising person."

"Why? Because I'm not a slut? Because I respect myself and others?" Good heavens. She sounded like a sanctimonious prude even to herself. "That came out more judgmental than I meant. Sorry."

He shrugged and began to amble in the direction of the hotel, still with one arm around her shoulders, fingers caressing her neck. Nothing in his posture or profile showed annoyance or frustration over her refusal.

She was impressed. Maybe she'd incorrectly concluded that Kam was immature. "We don't have to stop dancing now." Despite herself, her voice came out wistful.

He kissed her temple. "We can dance more tomorrow night."

As they stopped in front of the private elevator that went only to the penthouse floor, he kissed her again, then murmured in her ear, "Don't look now, but the mighty Hunter's at four o'clock."

"Your four o'clock or mine?"

"Mine, of course."

Of course, she thought. Just because Kam was a make-out artist didn't change his essential self-centeredness.

He plowed his fingers through her hair, pulling it out of her updo and using its length to tug her head back, exposing her throat. "Let's give her a show," he growled into her ear.

He sucked on her neck and she jerked away. "Don't you dare give me a hickey," she hissed.

Laughing, he shoved his key into the elevator, which opened. "You need to relax, my goddess." His cell phone rang, and he took the call.

She had a strong suspicion that his mind wasn't on business, since his eyes never left hers.

Relax, Kamar told himself three hours later. Though he'd taken a shower and stretched out in bed, his active mind refused to allow him to sleep. Instead, images and memories of Selina Carrington lingered.

She'd gone to a lot of trouble to prepare for their dinner. Her beautiful new dress, her coiffed hair, her makeup and manicure spoke of an infatuated woman. However, he'd seen that she wasn't so simple. There was something going on with this girl that was quite out of the ordinary.

She kissed like a courtesan, but claimed celibacy. He doubted she was untried—she was, after all, an American girl, and everyone knew that American virgins were rarer than diamonds.

Was she concerned because of the presence of her grandfather at the resort? Perhaps, but Jerome Carrington had tactfully absented himself for the entire evening. Kamar fleetingly wondered where the old man had been, then decided it really didn't matter. As long as Jerome wasn't around when Kamar made love to his granddaughter, the old fellow could take himself to perdition for all Kamar cared.

And he'd have her. It would take much effort, though. He knew women, and this one carried a shell like a hermit crab. Or perhaps like one of the tortoises that abounded in Zohra-zbel. They'd poke a head out and then retract, sometimes for weeks at a time.

He wanted to discover the woman within the shell, but what would it take to persuade Selina to abandon her shields? And why had she raised them in the first place?

Perhaps he could simply ask, but he doubted it. He'd already startled her, with his talk about the sophisticated games that men and women played, and his declaration that she wasn't happy. She hadn't liked that. Perhaps it had scared her, even, to know that someone had seen through her act.

But she was vulnerable, he'd discovered, vulnerable to tender kisses and the rapt attention he'd bestowed.

Selina was a challenge, a challenge too compelling

to ignore. The presence of her grandfather would add spice to the seduction. Kamar knew he was taking a risk, especially given the pesky reporter. What if the deception came to his father's notice?

The desk job.

Women always clad in enveloping veils.

No more gorgeous American girls.

Ah, but Selina...Selina was worth the risk. He promised himself that he'd have his goddess sometime within the next two weeks. He'd lay her bare and uncover her secrets, know her mysteries.

This little jaunt to Florida was proving much more interesting than Kamar had anticipated.

Chapter Seven

The next morning Kamar arose early, eager to resume the chase. As he dressed, he opened his drapes, and there she was, as though answering his prayer: Selina, all flaming hair, flashing white legs and bouncing breasts, jogging along the beach at the waterline, where the sand was packed firm.

"Good morning, my goddess," he said to himself, before going downstairs to intercept her. On the way, he bought small bottles of orange juice and water from one of the hotel shops. Marta Hunter was already there, purchasing several newspapers and a diet bar. Kamar masked his irritation, telling himself that this was an opportunity to again play Hunter like a fat stupid *huta*.

"Ms. Hunter," he said. "I trust that last night my intended and I supplied you with enough copy for your article?"

"Not nearly enough," Hunter said. Today the reporter was dressed more appropriately for the weather, in Bermuda shorts. Her bright fuchsia blouse would be easy to spot and evade, if necessary. Kamar smiled.

She continued, "I'm betting you'll marry while you're here. You know about the famous La Torchere spell, don't you?"

"Spell?"

"An unusual proportion of visitors to this resort marry. Right on that beach." She pointed, then patted a pocket, bulging with an oblong shape; her camera, Kamar supposed. "I'm wagering you'll be one of them."

"You'll lose that bet," Kamar said icily. The nerve of the woman, assuming that he'd elope as though ashamed of his fiancée. No. When he wed, it would be with the ceremonies befitting a prince of the Diamond Mountain.

Leaving Hunter behind, he went to meet Selina as she returned from her run. She'd stopped by one of the swimming pools and taken off her shirt, exposing the same lime-green halter top she'd worn yesterday. As he watched, she toed off her running shoes and socks, then pulled down her shorts.

His breath stuck somewhere between his chest and his throat, and it wasn't because of the humidity in the air. It was because Selina's body was surpassingly beautiful, and because she'd stripped down to her scanty bikini.

She stretched her arms above her head, then touched her toes with ease before placing her palms fully on the ground. Limber, he thought. Perfect. He liked the many positions of pleasure a limber bedmate could assume. He intended to enjoy every one of them inside Selina's luscious body.

Straightening, Selina twisted her torso from side to side, her breasts shifting with every movement.

Kamar's khaki shorts, though properly fitted, seemed to tighten. He pulled his shirt away from his chest while finding the shade of a tree. He wondered if he was wise to pursue Selina. *Father, desk job, veils. Remember?*

Selina dove into the water, shattering its turquoise stillness, which refracted into a million glittering shards, reflecting the morning sun. She stroked up and down the pool several times, her speed and vigor reflecting excellent fitness.

Kamar sighed. He loved American girls. Too bad he couldn't marry one, for no woman of his country would consider immodestly stripping down to underclothing and jumping into the water.

A family, complete with father, mother, babe in arms and a couple of toddlers carrying inflated water toys arrived. They took over a table near the pool.

Approaching the area, Kamar picked the top towel from one of the several stacks laid out. He met Selina at the shallow end, reaching to help her out. She took his offered hand with an almost dainty gesture and leaned on his arm as she stepped out of the pool. Her dripping hair soaked his shirt. He didn't care. It felt good, and her hand in his felt even better.

"Oh, isn't that cute," he heard the mother murmur. He assumed that one of her tykes had done something adorable, so he turned to look. To his surprise, the family was giving him and Selina identical warm smiles. Even the baby had a toothless, gummy grin for them.

Selina's pale skin flushed. She opened her mouth, no doubt to deliver one of her stinging put-downs, but before she could speak, he muttered, "Hunter's around."

She closed her lips with a snap, pressed them together, then said, "Already?"

"Already." He gave her the towel.

"Thank you." She wiped her face, then wrapped the towel around her hair. He led her to a lounge chair and offered her the water and the juice. She accepted the juice with a strained smile and tried to loosen its top with wet, slippery fingers. Without speaking, he took it, unscrewed it and handed it back before opening the water for himself.

As he sipped, he watched her drink, her white throat working. She tipped the bottle to get the last few drops. "My, that's good." She leaned back into the lounge chair with a satisfied sigh.

Kamar wondered if she sighed with such completion after the act of love, and what it would take to find out. Whether she knew it or not, Selina Carrington was no prude, but a very sensual woman faking chastity.

"Jerry's expecting us both for breakfast. Our suite, our treat." Though her smile flattered, she looked over his shoulder.

He pivoted to see Marta Hunter. After giving her a scowl, he smiled at Selina and said, "If that is the case, let us go." Just for the fun of it, he kissed her. "Good morning."

She kissed back. "And good morning to you. Sleep well?"

He hesitated. He couldn't tell her what he'd been thinking about all night, could he? "Fine. But it is always odd, getting used to a new bed."

They gathered her things and walked to the hotel, with Kamar feeling the stares of the family and of Hunter piercing him like arrows in the center of his back. He glanced at Selina, who said, "I didn't sleep a wink myself." Her smile was wan. "Considering how late we were up, I should have slept, but..." She shrugged.

He took out his card key and unlocked their private elevator. "It is a strange situation, is it not?"

Stepping into the elevator, she waited until it had closed. "You bet it is," she said fervently. "It's a combination of crazy and fun that I...I never..."

"We must figure out how to emphasize the fun, or the next two weeks will be unbearable."

"Maybe we can shorten this. I think that Grandpa Jerry will show you the multiple listing service print-outs this morning. Maybe you can pick one or two out. Make an offer on something." Her blue eyes pled, sending him messages at odds with the puckered nipples pricking her lime-green halter top.

Don't stare, he told himself. "Yes."

They arrived at the penthouse floor, and Selina opened the door of the Carringtons' suite.

"Ah! You're here!" Jerome Carrington greeted them with a broad smile. "I'll order breakfast. Sellie, your usual?"

"Yeah, thanks. Uh, I need to go shower the chlorine out of my hair." Selina left, barely managing to stop herself from slamming the door to her bedroom.

She locked the door—just in case—before retreating into her bathroom.

Why on earth had Kam gotten up so early and followed her outside? Couldn't she have a moment's peace?

She hadn't slept all night. She couldn't meditate. She couldn't run. She couldn't do anything without Kam Asad invading her thoughts or her personal space.

He was such a touchy-feely person, and behaving as though engaged meant a lot of touchy-feely stuff, not just an occasional kiss. Since yesterday his hands seemed to be on her constantly, and not just in the gentlemanly guise of helping her out, though he did plenty of that. If he opened a door for her, which he always did, he'd guide her through with a broad, warm palm on her waist or hip. If she walked on a set of stairs, he'd help her, even though the stairs might be shallow steps out of the swimming pool.

And so on. She'd found herself expecting his touch, welcoming it, even.

He'd gotten under her skin, engendered feelings she didn't want, an itchy twitchiness that could drive her straight to the loony bin. Why did he have to act so nice? She preferred her initial impression of him as an arrogant buffoon. She could take down a jerk without a second thought, but nice guys—or rather, guys who appeared to be nice—were another story. They presented questions like: How nice are they really? Is there a jerk beneath the nice-guy facade? And when would the jerk show up to crash the party?

Kam had facets she didn't want to acknowledge.

Last night he'd been sexy, attentive…overwhelming. This morning he'd been kind, thoughtfully bringing her a cool drink after her morning run. That wasn't the act of an arrogant buffoon.

In addition to the mysteries Kam presented, there was the problem of Marta Hunter. Selina brooded as she took off her new bikini, rinsed it in the sink, then got into the shower. She hoped she'd persuaded Prince Kamär to accelerate the home-buying process, but what could anyone do about that blasted reporter?

The family by the pool had been the last straw. *Cute,* the mom had murmured. Selina didn't aspire to cuteness. Cuteness was for children and teenagers, and her childhood memories were not happy ones.

She washed her hair, stepped out of the shower, dried off and braced herself for the challenge of another nerve-racking day in Prince Kamar's company. She didn't dawdle although she knew that Kam and Grandpa Jerry would still be gabbing in the suite's dining area. Kam might make her nervous, might engender all sorts of fantasies she didn't want, but she wasn't going to run or hide.

Besides, she was hungry. After dressing, she caught her breath, straightened her spine and left her room. As she'd surmised, Kam and Jerry were bent over piles of paper scattered over the dinette table, with Kam trying to choose one of the several opulent houses available for the ambassador's residence.

Listening with only half an ear—who cared where the ambassador lived?—Selina sat at the breakfast bar and poured herself coffee, found a croissant, ate some fruit. She'd read most of the *Washington Post* before loud, triumphant male voices pulled her out of the book section, in which she'd been reading a review of the latest Janet Evanovich title.

"What?" Folding the newspaper, she laid it aside.

"We found a place. A beautiful home. Come see, Selina. I must have my fiancée's approval." Waving a paper, Kam winked at her.

Jerry beamed. Did "Matchmaker, Matchmaker" play in his head, or was Pink Floyd's "Money" the tune turning him on?

"Okay, let's see," she said. Kam had picked a three-story brownstone in tony Georgetown. Selina tried to restrain a stab of jealousy, but she could work her butt off for ten thousand years and never be able to afford Georgetown. "Very nice. Are you going to make an offer?"

"Yes," Jerry said. "We'll give the seller seventy-two hours to consider it."

Glancing at Selina, Kam said, "I'll pay cash."

"But it's an out-of-state transaction with a foreign national," Jerry countered smoothly. Was he trying to delay the process, force them together for longer?

Selina frowned as her grandfather continued, "Kam, you have some papers to sign so I can fax your offer today. I'll prepare it immediately. After that, why don't you two throw Hunter off the track even more? If you can divert her, I'll go to the business center and get this going."

Still seated, Kam stretched out his legs beneath the table, smiling at her. "That means that you and I have the rest of the day together."

Chapter Eight

In her office, Merry Montrose cranked up the volume on her speakerphone so she could clearly hear her caller. Rick Barnett, an architect who'd submitted plans for a wedding chapel, had transmitted his ideas to her via e-mail. While they talked, she opened the file. When he finally stopped pitching her, she said, "This looks wonderful, Mr. Barnett."

"It does?"

"Yes. You're apparently a man of considerable ability. Why don't you come to La Torchere to survey the property? We'll be happy to pay your expenses. I believe your plans suit the site we've selected, but your personal inspection would be necessary before we finalize our contract, wouldn't it?"

"I'll come right out," Barnett said, sounding excited.

As Merry concluded the conversation, she wondered if Rick Barnett was married. If not, perhaps she'd be able to hook him up with one of the single women at the resort.

Not Selina Carrington, though. From what Merry had heard from the restaurant staff, Kam Asad and Selina Carrington could well be her twentieth couple. Twenty out of twenty-one!

Merry's heart beat fast. With the curse broken, she'd regain her young, beautiful persona, as well as her life as a princess.

No more aching joints! She'd appreciate that most of all.

Ready to go to lunch, she left her office to see Jerome Carrington approach the concierge desk. Just in case, she intercepted him before he made it to Lissa, her godmother. Close to breaking the curse, Merry wouldn't let Lissa throw a wrench in the works.

"How can I help you, Mr. Carrington?" Merry asked.

He waved a sheaf of papers. "I have to fax these to a real estate office in D.C."

"Oh?"

He lowered his voice. "Yes. It's a private deal between Sheik Kamar and me. Very private, if you know what I mean."

"I don't, but it's not my business. You can trust my discretion," Merry said. She glanced behind her at the business center door, aware of her godmother's presence. "Um, the business center is closed now, but I can personally take care of faxing these right away if you wish."

Carrington looked relieved. "Thank you. You know, I'm impressed by the level of service here."

Despite her loathing of the curse and everything that went with it, she preened. "We're very proud of La Torchere. Our goal is to provide a top-shelf, five-star-resort experience, and we believe that we deliver."

"You do," Carrington said. "By the way, I'll be at loose ends for a day or two after that fax goes through. What would you recommend by way of, um, diversion?"

His eyes twinkled. Was the man flirting with her? She gulped, then decided that if Carrington was ready for love, she'd find someone who'd oblige him.

Hadn't she just steered an attractive older lady to the Oasis pool for a swimming class? Perhaps Emma Forsythe and Jerome Carrington would become her final couple. Merry said, "We offer numerous diversions, Mr. Carrington. A number of our guests enjoy the water aerobics we offer in the Oasis pool. Why don't you try that this afternoon?"

"Sounds good." Jerome Carrington handed her his sheaf of papers and left, hopefully to go fall in love with Emma Forsythe.

Merry went behind the concierge desk to the resort's business center. With her godmother's gaze skewering her between the shoulder blades, she unlocked the business center and closed the door behind her.

As she examined the offer, anxiety overcame her in a sickening wave of self-doubt. The real estate deal between Carrington and Prince Kamar was proceeding at a much faster pace than she wanted. Surely they'd leave La Torchere once the deal was finalized, and if

Selina and Kamar hadn't tied the knot, Merry would
have to find another couple number twenty.

She had to fax the papers to the seller, as she'd
promised, but how could she slow down the rest of
the process?

Merry started to fax the papers to the number Carrington had specified. As the machine whirred, her
mind worked overtime.

She finished, and the fax spat out a report indicating
that the paperwork had been received by the seller's
fax. "Well, isn't that just wonderful," she muttered.

She glared at the machine with a fixed, intent expression. The seller would fax something back unless…

Pointing a finger, she intoned, "Fax machine, fax
machine, be not my bane."

What rhymed with bane? Crane, drain, main. She
struggled to create an effective couplet that would
work as a charm, then waved an imperious finger at
the fax. "Fax machine, stop here now. No more faxes
anyhow."

Pathetic. She grimaced.

As she waved her finger again, a young staffer
stepped into the room and froze in place, apparently
transfixed by the sight of her boss telling off a fax
machine with a pointing finger and a stern expression.

Merry snapped, "Are you lost?"

The staffer skedaddled.

Merry went to the coffeepot at the counter and
picked up three little blue packets of sweetener. After
opening the top of the fax, she ripped apart the packets and dumped the fake sugar into the machine's in-
nards.

Chapter Nine

After eating lunch at a poolside café, Selina, hand in hand with Kam, walked along a roofed colonnade lined with shops. She said to him, "Thanks for being, well, such a prince."

"Thanks for what? Lunch? Don't be ridiculous."

"Thanks for making an offer on a house so fast. You didn't do that because of me, did you?"

Tugging her hand, he wandered inside a shop that sold art glass. "Not entirely. I like the house, but I am mindful of our situation. Should word of my phony engagement reach my father's ears, the repercussions could be…uncomfortable."

"Oh?"

"Yes. He was quite displeased when *People* magazine—"

"Oh, yeah. That."

"Yes, that. I am not afraid of what Hunter may write. No one in Zohra-zbel reads her cage liner. But

if matters went further, there could be a problem.''
He stopped in front of a display of red and orange
bowls.

Each looked like the seething interior of a volcano.
Hot, violent and chaotic, but with a passion that fascinated. "Then we should limit this, um, game, as
much as possible.'' She ran a finger around the gold-
leaf rim of one bowl.

He smiled. "Should the seller accept the offer we
have made, there will be no further need for the deception. Does this bowl please you? I should like to
give you a gift.''

"That's nice of you, but I don't think I can get it
back to D.C. without breaking it.''

A saleswoman interposed, "We have guaranteed
shipping. But if you would like, we have smaller
pieces as well as a variety of art jewelry.'' She gestured toward a glassed-in case.

Kam frowned. "Should I give you a jewel, it will
surely come from our diamond mines.''

"You don't have to give me anything,'' Selina said.

"Sure he does.'' The saleswoman smiled and
glanced at Selina's hand. "I heard from my friends in
the restaurant that you're engaged. Without a ring, it's
just not real, is it?''

Selina caught Kam's eye. He looked as flabber-
gasted as she felt.

"I'm sorry.'' The saleswoman pressed a palm to
her forehead. Her cheeks had turned red. "That was
a very intrusive comment. Please forgive me.''

"No, you're right,'' Kam said.

Selina dragged him to a quiet corner of the shop

and murmured, "I don't want her pushing you into anything you don't want."

"I appreciate that, but perhaps she is right." He'd also dropped his voice. "Buying you a ring will solidify the deception. We can make sure Hunter sees it. Perhaps if she has something to take to her newspaper, she will leave us alone for a couple of days."

"By then we should have heard from the seller, and then it won't matter what she thinks anymore. That's not a bad idea, but what if it comes to your father's attention?"

"It won't. As I said, he doesn't read the *National Devourer.*"

"Okay, but don't get anything too expensive, okay?"

His face assumed a pharaoh's haughtiness. "I'll purchase a ring worthy of the intended bride of a prince of Zohra-zbel."

He stalked back to the jewelry display, Selina following.

"Let us see your wedding sets," he said.

"Oh, we don't have wedding sets in here," the woman said. "There's a more conventional jewelry store farther along. We carry art jewelry, one-of-a-kind pieces by local artists."

"Since my Selina is one of a kind, that is most appropriate."

Fifteen minutes later, Selina found herself wearing a swirl of gold and diamonds, with an astounding ruby at its core. Stupefied, she let Kam lead her out to the gardens.

The sun beat on the stone path, and he guided her along a shady trail that wound through lush undergrowth.

"No one has ever given me anything so beautiful before," she told him.

"It is but a bauble, no more than any lovely woman deserves. But you withhold so much of yourself. We men are mercenary. A giving woman encourages us to give."

"That's cold. You mean that I'd get more goodies if I fooled around more?"

He shrugged. "Yes."

"Cold and crass." She removed her hand from his.

"But true. I understand why you would not wish to be part of an exchange, but the game you play is still a mystery to me, my goddess."

"Game?"

"Dance-away lover, first sweet then remote, cutting then kind."

"I'm trying not to play that game with you. Right now we're playing Grandpa Jerry's game, and rather well, I think." She grinned at him.

"But I want to know you."

"You do? Why?"

"I like women," he said. "I like to know how they think and feel."

Women in general, she thought, not Selina in particular. She'd keep that in mind. "Oh, you're just trying to get me into bed. You know I don't sleep around."

"Why not?" His caressing fingers raised ripples of desire along her skin. "Your kiss has such promise.

Why do you fear to fulfill that promise—with me? Goddesses should be afraid of nothing.''

She opened her mouth, intending to deny her fear, but closed her lips before she said anything. She didn't want to lie. ''I'm not a goddess.''

''All women are goddesses, each in her own special manner. But some women hide their divinity, often out of fear. What frightened you, my Selina?''

''I'm not frightened,'' she snapped. ''Just wary.'' She stopped walking and sank down upon a nearby bench. Around her, tropical birds chirped, emitting weird cries. A nearby streamlet trickled musically over stones, cooling the area despite the sun slanting through the trees. Shade dappled the bench, her legs, Kam's dark hair. A shaft of light slipped through the foliage, striking flames in the red heart of the ruby she wore.

''Wary, then. Why?''

''I had some bad experiences,'' she said, wondering how much she should tell him. She wasn't ashamed of what had happened, but she had no reason to shock Kam.

''It would be surprising if you didn't have at least one bad experience with a man. Men are dogs.''

''I think so, but I'm surprised to hear you say so. On top of that, you're the alpha dog, right?'' Maybe that was why he bothered her. Wealthy, handsome and powerful, Kam was a dominant male to the core. All that masculine potency wrapped up in one package was probably what had gotten to her, sliding under her skin to make her itchy and twitchy when he was around.

"No." He grinned. "Not at home. In Zohra-zbel, I am prince beta. My father is the alpha, of course, and my older brother will succeed him to the throne."

"Huh. Does that bother you?"

"Not at all. He is much wiser and more responsible than I am. I am not alpha or beta or anything else remarkable. I am just a man who loves women."

She eyed Kam, unable to figure him out. Nice guy or arrogant buffoon? Frustrated alpha or happy second son?

"Many younger brothers are jealous of the older. He gets to be king one day, tell you what to do, and boss you around. That doesn't bother you?"

"Oh, no. I have all the fun, but Denya must one day carry the weight of the crown. He trains daily for the responsibility, while I travel the world, buy properties and date exotic American women." He winked at her. "But we were speaking of your situation, not of mine."

Damn. Here was that itchy, twitchy feeling again, crawling up her spine, sharpening her words. "All right, fine. My father died when I was twelve."

"I am sorry. As stern as my father is, I depend upon his wisdom. That is a great loss."

"Thank you. It changed everything."

"My mother did not survive my birth. I suppose I was the death of her."

"So you…" She lifted an eyebrow. "Who raised you?"

"My father, the king, of course, with assistance from relatives. Though I must admit that nannies and maids did most of the work."

"Interesting," Selina said, thinking that because Kam's early contacts with women were all with servants, he'd developed the attitude that females were inferior, objects for his use or amusement. That made a lot of sense, considering his reputation.

He grinned. "My mother left me an unusual legacy, though. My name, Kamar, means moon in the language of my people. Denya is named after the earth. I suppose I am fated to orbit my brother."

"A fanciful woman. My name also means the moon."

"Another connection between us. Tell Hunter that we are clearly destined to be together. That is the kind of detail *National Devourer* readers, um, devour."

She chuckled. "How come you know so much about her readers?"

"Never mind that. We were talking about you, weren't we?"

Her jaw tensed, but she said, "After my father died, my mother remarried a, well, a dog." Rage thickened her throat, and she swallowed. "He tried to rape me when I was fifteen."

"How? How could your family allow that?" Kam grabbed her hand.

Selina really didn't want Kam freaking out about it. She shrugged, trying to fake flippancy. "One day I was watching television and studying. It was in the afternoon, and I got drowsy. I lay down on the couch and nodded off. I woke up when there was this weight on me, and it was *him*. He was lying on top of me, sticking his tongue down my throat and ripping at my jeans."

Kam said something in Arabic that sounded really nasty. "Go on."

She wiggled her fingers to loosen his painfully tight grip. "Well, I, um, kneed him where it counts, if you know what I mean, and scratched and bit. I wasn't really hurt, but…"

"You *were* hurt. He hurt your female soul and scared the passion out of you."

Her spine snapped straight. "I'm not hurt and I'm not scared. I'm selective, that's all. You got a problem with that?"

"Of course not." He drew back, but didn't release her hand. "What happened after that despicable dog of a stepfather, may his entrails rot while he still lives, touched you with violence?"

"This is really the worst part." She fiddled with Kam's fingers. "My mother threw me out."

"*What?* Why?"

"She chose her husband over me." With effort, she kept her voice flat.

"A most unnatural parent."

Selina shook her head. "She had a new baby, and she couldn't face what would happen if she left. She'd be a single mom with a teenager and a newborn. That would have been tough."

"Stop making excuses for her."

"I'm trying to forgive her."

"Some acts are unforgivable."

"Maybe." She shrugged. "I think that what made it worse is that I wasn't a particularly attractive child."

Kam lost his frown, and one brow lifted.

"No, really. I was one of those redheaded, tubby kids with freckles and baby fat. So I never had a boyfriend or anything, and all of a sudden, when I turned fifteen, I got all this male attention. It felt like, you know, fake."

"You're a beautiful woman." Kam's tone was prosaic. "Men are attracted to beautiful women."

"But I wasn't beautiful inside, you see? I didn't know that."

"Do you know that now?"

"I...I'm not really sure. Sometimes I feel like that same lost kid, you know, missing her father, distrusting her mom and afraid of her stepdad."

"No child should have to live with fear." Kam's fists were clenched, his muscles tight.

She touched him on the shoulder. "It's okay. It's over. It's been over for years." She rubbed his shoulder until the sinews beneath her fingers relaxed.

He shrugged. "If you say so. When was the last time you saw your mother and her husband?"

"Audra, my mother, brought my little brother to the graduation ceremony when I finished business school. He—Nicky—was about six, and the cutest little boy. They ate dinner with Grandpa Jerry and me. But it was weird, because, well, I didn't have anything to say to my mother, and Nicky acted as though I was a stranger, not his sister. He'd heard about me, but we hadn't seen each other since he was a baby."

"Have you since seen your brother?"

She sighed. "Every once in a while. He's only eight, so he can't travel alone to D.C. to see us. When he turns ten, Jerry and I plan to ask my mom if she'll let him visit every couple of months.''

"Have you seen the stepfather?"

"No, he's smart enough to stay away. Jerry had once told him he'd beat him up if he ever saw him again."

"Intelligent of your stepfather to take that threat seriously. In the place of your father, it is your grandfather's duty to protect your honor."

She gurgled with laughter. "I suppose you could say that."

"So, I gather that when your mother made you leave, you went to live with Jerome?"

"Yeah. I went to a police station, and they brought Donald—my stepfather—in for questioning and called Jerry. Donald denied everything, of course, but they made him go into a treatment program. I never went back, though. Grandpa Jerry's taken care of me ever since."

"He has done a fine job." Kam's voice warmed. "You are an amazing person, Selina. See why I call you a goddess? You are so beautiful, so normal and healthy, even after what you have been through."

"Thanks." She couldn't meet his eyes. She wasn't sure that she was really normal or healthy, but she felt that she'd revealed enough of herself for one day.

"Let's walk some more." He gently tugged her hand, and when she stood, he draped his arm over her shoulders, pulling her in for a hug. "Yours is a sad tale."

She pursed her lips. "I guess so, but I'm lucky. He didn't hurt me physically. I had somewhere to go. A lot of teens in my situation don't have anyone. They end up on the streets, pregnant and alone.''

"Now much is clear to me. I will respect your boundaries. Until you are ready for me, I will not push you.''

"What do you mean, ready?''

He stopped and pulled her close, until his hard, hot body pressed against her. "I think you know exactly what I mean.''

She lost her breath. "I, uh, I... You mean, you want me, but *I* have to—''

"Exactly. *You* have to. Not me.'' Releasing her, he walked, her hand still captured in his.

"Huh.'' This was unique. All the men Selina had dated had tried to get her into bed, then left when they didn't succeed after the first few evenings, as though a couple of dinners entitled them to possess her body, her heart and her soul. Kam sounded as though he wanted to stick around, wait for her to decide when she was ready.

Selina strolled toward the Oasis swimming pool, Kam close and attentive. Unburdening herself to him had felt...right, as though she'd talked with a trusted friend. She literally felt brighter, as though she shone, and lighter on her feet.

Not that talking really changed anything, of course. She'd talked to a lot of people about what had happened to her—the police, Jerry, therapists, friends. Telling Kam didn't make any difference. But she wondered if they'd see each other again after this vacation was over. After exposing so much of herself to him, it would be odd to lose touch completely.

"Maybe after this is over, we can have dinner sometime," she said, testing.

"Especially if I decide to take that ambassadorship. Selina, I meant what I said. I can wait for my goddess to be ready."

"You seem very confident." Too bad she wasn't. She hadn't felt much for any man...until Kam, and she really wasn't sure of him. She might never be.

"I am confident in you, in your passion."

"My what?"

"Your passion. You do not see yourself as passionate, but you are." He lifted her left hand, kissing the ruby on her fourth finger. "Your heart has the fire of this stone. That is why I picked it for you."

"I...I...what?"

Kam laughed. "Strange, the illusions we cherish, hmm? I have the illusion that everyone loves me, which you challenged. You believe that your stepfather frightened the passion out of you forever, and I intend to destroy that belief."

"I told you, I'm not scared."

"If you say so." He gave her a smug smile. "I believe I am right and that I will succeed."

She was about to argue with him some more when Jerry, surrounded by a bevy of women, caught her attention. Selina stopped so suddenly that Kam bumped into her. She pointed toward the swimming pool. "Look at that."

Her grandfather sat under an umbrella next to an attractive older lady. Nearby, a younger woman tucked her fair hair beneath a hat. A few feet away, sprawled in a lounge chair, Marta Hunter tapped on a laptop computer.

"Oh, your grandfather has found himself lady friends." With Selina's hand still in his, Kam headed toward Grandpa Jerry. "Excuse us," Kam said to the women.

Jerry looked up. "Well! What have you two young people been up to?"

"We, um, we bought a ring." Selina held out her hand, aware of Hunter's scrutiny.

"Not a diamond? I'm surprised," Jerry said.

"I felt that a ruby would symbolize our passion," Kam said with a wink and a nod toward Hunter.

"How romantic." The older lady glanced at the ring, then at the younger, fair-haired woman. Selina wondered which female Grandpa Jerry was interested in.

"This is Emma Forsythe and her daughter, Cindy," Jerome said.

"Cynthia," Emma Forsythe said.

"Pleased to meet you," Selina said. She glanced at Cynthia, whose face reddened.

Selina experienced a flash of sympathy toward the girl, whose mother might as well have "battle-ax" tattooed on her forehead. "Hey, Cynthia," Selina said. "Want to have dinner with us tonight?"

"She wouldn't want to intrude," Emma said.

"She wouldn't be intruding, nor would she be out of place if she went parasailing with us tomorrow," Kam said.

"Parasailing? This is the first I've heard about para-sailing." Selina smiled at Kam.

"Oh, I couldn't do that," Cynthia said. "That sounds scary."

Wimp, Selina thought. She squared her shoulders. "It sounds fun to me. Let's do it."

Kam grinned at Selina. "Sometimes taking chances can be good."

Chapter Ten

"I don't understand why you won't be reasonable about this." Joyce Phipps-Stover slammed a drawer shut on a frothy pile of pink lace lingerie. "You've seen my ledgers. The economy's lousy, and I can't sell the shop without losing over a hundred grand in loans. Personal loans, Brian. I love you, but I won't screw over my friends by declaring bankruptcy just because you're a stubborn jerk."

Brian, her husband of six months, threw his empty suitcase into the closet with a crash. "I'm settled in at Reno High."

"There are plenty of teaching jobs in the St. Paul-Minneapolis area."

"I'm head of the English department and have tenure. I'm not about to give up what I've worked for since I was seventeen to move to Antarctica."

"St. Paul isn't Antarctica. Granted, it can be cold in the winter, but so is northern Nevada." She'd tried living in Reno and hated it. "What do you see in that place, anyhow? It's a horrible little town masquerading as a city. It's dirty, dusty and downright tawdry. Strip clubs and casinos…ick."

"That's just downtown. Suburban Reno's a good place to raise children."

Her fury built. "I wouldn't bring that up if I were you." At age twenty-four, she had plenty of time to bear children. She didn't want to get pregnant until she was about thirty, but for whatever reason, Brian wanted to have babies right away. He'd even thrown out her birth control pills, which had outraged her.

"Reno's my home." Brian stalked through the villa to its living room.

She followed. "Well, it's not mine." After he'd tossed her pills, she'd flown back to St. Paul, to her home and her life. She'd slipped right back in; returning to St. Paul had felt like putting on a beloved old sweater. Fortunately, her competent assistant had run the shop for the few months she'd been in Reno.

"That's it in a nutshell, isn't it?" Brian flung open the villa's front door and left without bothering to close it behind him.

The sound of the door smashing against the wall reverberated through the villa. Despairing, Joyce sank down on the cushy sofa and assessed her surroundings. La Torchere was synonymous with luxury, and the villas were the crème de la crème of the resort. Set at the edge of the beach, they featured full views of the ocean, complete privacy and every amenity she could think of…except a reasonable attitude from the man she'd married. The sumptuous villa, with its ivory brocade couches, polished marble floors and enormous picture windows, contrasted with the bleakness in her heart.

She looked through the open doorway to the beach, the same beach where she and Brian had spoken vows of love just six months before.

Ironically enough, another couple stood there, he in a tux, she in a long white gown, with a minister and a small crowd of onlookers. Strange, she thought, the number of couples marrying at La Torchere. Who would have thought that steamy southwest Florida was a destination for romance?

Her first inclination was to run outside screaming *Stop! Stop!* Instead, she went to the kitchen to brew a strong cup of coffee.

She and Brian had both hoped to rediscover their love and the reasons they'd married by coming to La Torchere. Unfortunately, nothing had gone as planned; with their commitment forgotten and their marriage in a shambles, they'd argued for nearly all of their stay. Not even the helpful interference of the manager, Merry Montrose—who obviously had a penchant for matchmaking—could help.

Exhausted emotionally as well as physically, Joyce needed high-quality, high-octane brew, and fast. She'd brought her own espresso from The Ground Bean, her coffeehouse, and knew it was just the ticket. She found a coffeemaker on the counter and filters nearby. But after she filled the water reservoir and put coffee in the basket, the thing didn't start.

Maybe it wasn't plugged in. She flipped a light

switch so she could see behind the machine, but the overhead didn't come on.

Damn. Was every electrical connection in the place burned out?

Why not? Burnout seemed a fitting analogy to her marriage.

With a sigh she reached for a phone to call the front desk for help.

Scant minutes later, a knock at the door heralded the repair person, an attractive blond man, dressed in the same garb many resort employees wore: a teal polo shirt and khaki shorts. The tag on his shirt read Alec.

Joyce lifted a hand to her hair, pushed it back behind her ears and smiled. She didn't intend to cheat on her husband, even if he was an untrustworthy jerk, but it sure helped her morale to have a good-looking man around. She was glad she'd changed into a bikini with a see-through cover-up.

"The sockets seem to be burned out in the kitchen," she told him, leading him inside the villa.

"That's what my work order says." The repairman's blue eyes twinkled in his tanned face. "I'll just check the circuit breakers."

As he opened a panel hidden inside one of the cupboards, he said, "Someone's getting married out front, and there's another wedding right after that. I've seen a couple dance on the beach every night. What is it with this place?"

Joyce crossed her arms over her chest. "I don't know, but love seems to be in the air around here. Too bad it's limited to this island."

Alec cast her a surprised glance, but didn't ask any questions. Tactful, she thought. She appreciated that.

"We got married here, too," she said.

"Oh? Back for a second honeymoon?"

"Sort of." She giggled nervously.

"Sounds like fun." He flipped the panel closed with a snap. "Okay, everything should work now."

Joyce fiddled with the coffeemaker, which hissed as coffee began to drip into the glass pot. She sighed with relief and offered Alec a cup of coffee.

Later, after her husband had returned and they'd made up—sort of—she and Brian ate dinner in the kitchen of their villa. Through the window, she saw one of the couples Alec had mentioned, dancing on the sand.

Few pleasures equaled the joy of holding Selina in his arms. As they danced on the beach in the moonlight, Kamar lowered his head to nuzzle her hair. Tonight she'd let it flow freely along her exquisite neck and over her shoulders, and he'd discovered he loved to play with the silky strands.

As their time together continued, he'd noticed that she'd become more relaxed around him. They touched and kissed frequently, with Selina now initiating caresses. Even better, she'd spoken openly with him about her private pain, as though he were a trusted confidant.

Now she said, "I want to apologize to you for the way I treated you when we met. I was wrong about you."

"So I am not an arrogant buffoon?" He grinned at her. "And everyone does love me?"

"Well, you have your moments. You're more complicated than I thought."

"Me? I am not complicated. Women are complicated. I am a man, and men are easy."

"Yeah, they're dogs, or so I hear."

"Woof." He bent his head and nibbled on her throat, then kissed the spot he'd savaged. When he blew on the dampness, she quivered in his arms.

Her vulnerability heightened her allure, as did her contrasts. Her uninhibited kisses showed she'd had enough sexual experience to be interesting, and yet she did not give herself often or lightly. He appreciated that. When they finally came together, their affair would be passionate, not casual or empty.

He wondered how he could have her, discreetly and privately. Not at La Torchere, not with Jerome Carrington and Marta Hunter around.

As they danced, part of Kamar's mind began composing a letter to his father accepting the ambassadorship from Zohra-zbel to the United States. He could easily imagine Selina's naked body gracing a big bed in the ambassador's residence.

Chapter Eleven

Ignoring the ache from her sore, arthritic hip, Merry Montrose hurried along the garden path, trying to keep Kamar Asad and Selina Carrington within earshot. These young people don't appreciate their good health, she was thinking. When they're my age—

She stopped herself short, remembering that she *was* their age, though trapped in an old broad's body. But not for long, she promised herself.

Nothing wrong with her hearing, fortunately....

Rats and monkeys. They were planning to go parasailing! No, no, no. That was all wrong. She didn't want one of them flying through the air while the other waited on the beach. She wanted them together, falling in love and getting married.

But what would stop them?

Tipping back her head, she scrutinized a small, puffy cloud leisurely floating high in the blue, blue sky. She smiled at it, wiggling her left index finger.

The cloud puffed up a little more.

Merry increased the speed and diameter of her circular finger wiggle. The little cloud became a big cloud, crossing the sun.

Ducking behind a bush, she stretched her arms above her head and murmured, "Little cloud, you've made me proud. Give us rain, make us…make us…"

Make us what? Why couldn't she think of a decent rhyme for rain? She rubbed her aching hip. Pain came first to mind, but pain was bad.

Drain? With her bad luck, all the drains in the resort would flood. Brain? Show us your brain?

To heck with it. "Just give us some rain, all right?" she snapped.

The cloud obliged with a soft, misty drizzle.

Not bad, she thought, considering that her spell wasn't worthy of even an apprentice little witchie. Continuing along the path that Selina and Kamar had taken, Merry hoped that her meager spell-casting abilities would be enough.

Selina lifted her face to the heavens. "It's raining, Kam," she breathed. "Maybe there'll be a rainbow."

He slipped his arm around her. "But no parasailing. What, then, do you want to do today?"

"Well, it can't be anything outdoors."

"I can think of something to do indoors. In my suite. In bed."

She scowled. "You know my views on casual sex."

"It's not casual. We're engaged."

"And that would be soooo fun with my grandfather around."

"He's playing with Emma." Kam nuzzled her neck.

She giggled. "How about we take the ferry to town, do some sight-seeing, shopping?"

"Lunch?"

"Sure."

"Let's also take a drive. I rented a Porsche at the airport that will bring tears to your pretty blue eyes." He took her arm in a warm, possessive grip.

"Why would you want me to cry?"

"So I can kiss away your delicious tears and offer you the comfort of my manly arm." He winked.

She sniffed. "Why are you being so romantic?"

"We're engaged. You're beautiful. And that pest from the *National Devourer* is behind us. Bloody hell," he added under his breath.

Selina turned. "So she is. I also see the resort manager. I figured the show couldn't be for me." She shook her elbow, trying to get free.

Kam resisted. "Oh, but it is. Remember, you're beautiful."

She sniffed again.

His smile flattered. "Please don't tell me that you're one of those phony, modest girls, or a painfully insecure neurotic."

"I plead guilty. I am a painfully insecure neurotic and proud of it."

"Proud?"

"I come by my neuroses honestly."

His face fell. "Yes, you did." He'd dropped his

bantering tone. "I apologize. I shouldn't have teased you."

"It's all right. I've learned to live with it."

"Live with it? Perhaps. You survived by growing a shell like a dinosaur egg. But beneath, as you say, you're still a frightened kid."

He's listening to me, she thought. This is good. "Yep, that's about the size of it." She managed a cocky tilt of her chin.

Kam draped a friendly arm over her shoulders. "Well, I know what kids like."

"What?" she asked with suspicion.

He grinned. "Fast cars."

She grinned back. "Let's go upstairs and change."

"I like this bikini," he said, turning her around.

"What's so special about it? I've been wearing it all week."

"Do you hear me complaining? It shows lots of your skin."

"Oh, there's nothing unusual about my skin."

He squeezed her closer and bent his head to nibble on her earlobe. "Yes, there is. It belongs to a goddess."

Laughing, she shook her head as they entered the hotel. "You don't miss a chance, do you?"

To Selina's dismay, a bug-green P.T. Cruiser followed Kam's Porsche onto the ferry. A familiar but unwelcome figure sat behind the wheel. "What's she doing here?" she demanded of Kamar.

He glanced in his rearview mirror. "She is doing her job."

"Why do we have to be her job?"

"It's me, goddess, not you. I apologize."

"You don't need to apologize." She lifted her chin. "I refuse to let her spoil our day."

"That's the spirit!" Kam set the parking brake and got out of the car.

Selina fiddled with her seat belt, wondering if he'd open her door.

He did, asking, "Has the safety belt broken?"

Caught. She blushed. "No, I'm just a little fumble fingered this morning."

"Then fumble with my fingers." He caught her hand, casting a glance at the green car behind them. He swung Selina into his arms. "Let's give the old witch a little kissy face."

"Sure." Selina lightly rubbed her lips on his, keeping eye contact even when he slid his hand into her hair to bring her closer, deepening the kiss. He slipped his arms around her waist beneath her T-shirt.

More delightful shivers. She could get addicted to this man if she wasn't careful.

Before she was quite ready to stop, he released her. Despite her determination to not get involved, she felt a little…bereft when he let her go.

His dark eyes smiled. "Let's go topside and get a coffee."

After the ferry docked in town, Kam drove Selina to the city center. There, clustered around a central square, were the county government buildings as well as a museum and shops.

Selina consulted a tour guide she'd snagged on the

ferry. "It says here that the city hall, which also functions as the county seat, is a historic building dating from 1809 and renovated in the 1930s as a Works Project Administration program."

"Let's go in." Kam held open one of city hall's carved double doors.

Selina stepped inside. "Oh, look at this." The walls were covered by detailed murals depicting the history of Loveland County.

A flash distracted her, and she turned. Marta Hunter stood in the doorway, lowering her camera.

Irritation scraped Selina's nerves. Advancing, she snapped, "Are you stalking us?"

Hunter shrugged. "You're news. And a shot of the prince and his fiancée applying for a marriage license could be worth a lot."

"We aren't here to pad your wallet." Selina planted her hands on her hips. "Would you mind leaving us alone? How can I get to know this man if you're constantly on our butts?"

Without answering, Hunter slunk around Selina to a bench, evidently planning to linger.

Kam said to Selina, "What happened to your PR? That wasn't very diplomatic."

"There's a time for everything, even rudeness, and I am not getting a marriage license. That's going too far."

"Just getting the application? That would convince her that we're serious. Perhaps she would then let us alone."

Selina eyed Hunter. "Maybe you're right. It has to be filled out and sent back in, doesn't it?"

They went in to the county recorder's office. After they showed their IDs, a clerk typed their names onto the form and gave it to Selina. As she left, she marched over to Hunter and waved it. "Here it is! Satisfied?"

"Thank you, Lord above." Hunter whipped out her camera and took a photo.

"Don't thank Him," Selina snapped. "God has nothing to do with this. As far as we're concerned, you can go straight to hell and check in with your boss, the devil. Are you going to let us alone now?"

"At least until my story's filed." Hunter dashed toward the door.

Chapter Twelve

With Hunter busy filing her story, Selina and Kam spent a pleasant day touring south Florida. Kam hadn't lied about his rental car. Selina, who didn't own a car and hadn't known how to drive a manual transmission, had spent the afternoon learning. After an hour, she liked the Porsche so much that she and Kam had to negotiate to divide driving responsibilities.

They returned to the resort well after sundown. To their surprise, a small welcoming committee stood on the dock to greet them: Marta Hunter, camera in hand, and another woman Selina didn't recognize.

"*Ixzit.*" Kam braked, then stopped the Porsche.

"What? What does izzit mean?"

"*Ixzit.* It is a mild expletive, like your darn or damn. But never mind that. Look there."

"What?" Selina asked, craning her head to look past him to the pair on the wharf. "Marta Hunter here to say hello? Oh well. I'm kinda getting used to her. Besides, I've had such a good day I refuse to get upset about her.''

''I am not bothered by Hunter, but that other lady is the resort manager.''

''Why would she be here?'' Selina's breath caught in her throat. ''Do you suppose that there's something wrong with Grandpa Jerry?''

Kam unrolled his window. ''Ms. Montrose, what a, uh, pleasant surprise. All is well with Mr. Carrington?''

''I believe so,'' the older woman said. ''I last saw him eating supper with Emma Forsythe.''

Selina noticed that Ms. Montrose held herself stiffly, as though her back or her hips pained her. Poor lady, Selina thought. Aging must be hell if you're in poor health.

The resort manager continued, ''I heard from Marta Hunter that you picked up a marriage license at the courthouse today.''

''Just a formality.'' Kam shrugged.

''Would you mind telling me if you signed it?''

''No.'' Kam handed it over.

''Can you do so?'' She handed it back with a pen.

''What for?'' Selina asked.

''It doesn't mean anything unless it's signed.''

''It's not supposed to mean anything,'' Selina murmured.

Kam's cell phone rang. As he pulled it out and thumbed a button, he said, ''Just sign the wretched thing, all right? Perhaps then all these people will leave us alone.'' Kam signed, then handed the paper and the pen to Selina while Hunter's camera flashed. He then returned to his phone call, conducting a voluble exchange in Arabic.

While Selina signed her name, she noticed that the resort manager had become officious and more than a little irritating. What was the deal, anyhow?

Finally, she and Kam—still on his cell phone— finished answering a bunch of annoying questions, signed everything, and they were free to go. When he'd finished his call, she asked, "What the heck was all that about, anyhow?"

"The phone call? They just wanted to know—"

"No, not the phone call," she said, exasperated.

"Oh, Montrose and Hunter." He put the Porsche into gear. "I'm not sure. Security, I would think. Since 9/11 you Americans have correctly instituted many new security procedures."

"Jerry and I didn't go through that when we came here," Selina grumbled.

"Perhaps they forgot, and are now making up for it."

"You're probably right. Hey, I'm hungry. How about some dinner?"

Kamar looked her over. "You're not exactly dressed for it." She was wearing her floppy canvas hat, a T-shirt, wrinkled capris and her three-inch platform sandals. He had to admit that the shoes were growing on him.

"Yeah," she said. "Like you're so formal."

"It's the Marlins' cap," Kamar said, stopping in front of the hotel.

"Or the Florida Is for Lovers T-shirt."

"I think it is most appropriate." Kamar winked at Selina as a valet opened her door.

She waited until Kam walked around the car to her, then asked, "How about a burger by the pool? Then we don't have to change."

"But you have looked so beautiful for our dinners."

"I'm tired of playing dress-up every night."

"It is so flattering, the trouble you go to."

"It's because I'm insecure."

"You shouldn't be." He took her hand as they went into the hotel.

"Maybe not. Um, how about that burger?"

"A burger it is, then our walk."

"We can dance, too. Think they'll play 'Unforgettable' for us?"

The next day dawned sunny and hot. After Kam took Selina parasailing, which she found exhilarating but exhausting, they went to their respective suites to relax before dinner.

She showered and put on a terry robe. Before she lay down for a much-needed rest, she looked out the window to see Jerry seated next to Emma Forsythe on lounge chairs by the pool. Both sipped umbrella drinks and appeared delighted with life.

"Good for you, Grandpa Jerry," Selina murmured as she curled up on the sofa for a nap.

She was roused by banging on the suite door. Blinking, she raised her head. Long sunbeams slanted through the window, so she guessed it was late in the afternoon. She staggered to the door and, recognizing Kam's voice calling her name, opened it.

"Wha—what?" She rubbed her temples. Could she be hallucinating? Kam, clad only in boxer shorts, was at her door, hair standing on end. The naked chest was good; his frantic disarray wasn't.

He waved a paper. "We could be in a lot of trouble."

"What? Did the deal fall through?"

"This doesn't have anything to do with the house. This is about us."

"Us?" Selina grabbed the paper. It was the same one they'd picked up at the courthouse the day before, but now the marriage license was stamped FILED in big, official looking letters.

"*Ixzit.* Where did you get this?"

"It arrived by special messenger a few minutes ago." He strode into the suite, pacing back and forth. "We're married."

"No way."

"Look at it! It's a Florida marriage license. We both signed it and now it's filed."

Willing herself to remain in control, Selina examined the document. Her heart lurched. "You're right. Check this out. A judge made it official after a notary signed it. Who's Meredith Montrose?"

"She's the resort manager. What does she have to do with this?"

"She's the notary." Selina caught her breath, a little dizzy. "That witch. She must be in league with Hunter. Hunter always seems to know what we're doing and where we're going. Montrose must be telling her. Do you remember that they were both at the dock last night, asking questions and taking pictures?''

"They married us without our knowledge or consent." Kam slammed a fist into the nearest wall.

"Damn. What if your father finds out?"

"Exactly what I was thinking."

"We have to get this annulled as soon as possible."

He visibly calmed. "Yes, we can do that, can't we?"

"Sure. It's no big deal, is it?"

His gaze shifted. "I suppose not."

"It really isn't. It's a, a mix-up, that's all. We'll get it straightened out in the morning."

"Yes, you are right." Kam backed out of the suite. "I will skip dinner with you tonight, Selina, all right? I will spend the time checking on how to get this annulled."

"Wait! Tomorrow's Saturday. Nothing will be open. And, until the house deal's done, maybe we shouldn't start any paperwork."

He paused. "That is so. The positive aspect is that no one will suspect that I am buying the ambassador's residence. But I must think on how to handle this. I am not hungry for dinner, Selina. I will see you later, perhaps."

Kamar left, wondering if Selina or her grandfather had anything to do with what had happened, but immediately dismissed the possibility that she was involved. He'd come to know Selina and her moods. Though she liked to play games, flirt and tease, she was incapable of this brand of deception. She'd looked truly startled, even a little shaky, when confronted with the document.

Her grandfather, though…Kamar brooded. He wouldn't be surprised if the old man had helped that pair of witches, Hunter and Montrose, to create this fiasco. Jerry had initially suggested the fake engagement, hadn't he? And then persuaded his granddaughter and Kamar to take part in it.

Returning to his suite, Kamar chewed on his lower lip. He'd been a fool, sucked into a scam that was very serious. He might be able to feign a casual attitude about this unexpected marriage to Selina, but in his life, marriage was a serious business. Kamar remembered when his brother had become betrothed to a young Saudi princess, Amira, who'd brought wealth and connections to the House of Zohra-zbel. The negotiations had taken more than a year, and the wedding had been a major event in the political lives of both nations.

Aware he was a valuable commodity to his country, Kamar expected a similar hubbub to surround his nuptials, though not at the level that had attended his brother's wedding. But this unplanned union with Selina Carrington could spoil his value as a marriage prospect to many of the notoriously selective Arabian royals.

How could he, in all honesty, conceal this disaster from his family?

He couldn't. Even if he wanted to, this event was of sufficient magnitude that after Hunter broke the story, it would be picked up by the major wire services. Though Zohra-zbel was a tiny country tucked high in the Atlas Mountains of north Africa, the news would surely reach his homeland.

Best to tell his father in person, rather than allowing him to learn of it second- or third-hand. Considering the possible consequences, Kamar winced. Heaven only knew how the king would react. The desk job and the veils would be minor repercussions; nevertheless, he had to be honest with his father and brother. Then everyone could consider how best to manage the situation.

Reaching for his ever-present cell phone, Kamar began to make arrangements to return to his country the next day.

Chapter Thirteen

After Kam left, Selina pushed still-damp hair out of her eyes and tried to wrap her mind around the situation.

She was married.

Still fuzzy-brained from her nap and the stunning news that Kam had delivered, she stood on shaky legs and wandered to her bathroom. She stared into the mirror at her wan face, flushed with a little sunburn and more than a little fear.

She was married. To Kam. To Kamar ibn-Asad, prince of Zohra-zbel. *People* magazine's sexy sheik.

A giggle escaped her, and she clamped a hand over her mouth. If she stifled herself, maybe she could stifle the hysteria rising inside her.

She was married.

She took a deep breath, expelled it, then another and another. As oxygen flooded her, she calmed. She felt the floor beneath her bare feet, the coolness of the marble countertop under her palms.

She'd be okay. This wasn't the worst thing that had happened to her, not remotely. No one had died. No one had attacked her. No one had thrown her out of her home. She had a place to sleep. She had Grandpa Jerry. She had a job and a nice studio apartment. She was okay.

And to prove it, she was going to put on her best dress and get some dinner. Just because Kam was a wimp about this and was going to hide out in his suite didn't mean that Selina would hide. Even though the news had twisted her guts into a knot, she was going to get dinner.

She didn't want to take the time to dry her hair, so she put the damp mass on top of her head and secured it with a clip. She found the red feathery dress and slipped it on, then headed out.

She didn't see Jerry anywhere, which bothered her a little. He was usually there for her, and without Jerry and Kam, who'd been her companions while at La Torchere, she felt a little bereft and at loose ends.

She went to the seaside lounge, where Janis tended bar. Choosing a couple of cashews from a bowl of mixed nuts, Selina waited until Janis had finished with other customers.

"Mazeltov." Janis reached under the bar and withdrew a bottle of champagne. "I heard you tied the knot today."

"Um, thanks." Selina crunched a nut between her back teeth to hide her extreme discomfiture.

"Where's the groom?" Janis popped open the champagne and poured Selina a glass.

Picking it up, she shrugged. "Primping for the wedding night, I guess."

Janis grinned. "Life surely is interesting. I could have sworn when the two of you met, you couldn't stand each other."

"He's nicer than he seems at first glance," Selina said lamely.

"Must be. Hey, I have an idea. There are little bowers—secluded clearings along the shoreline—with cabanas, hammocks, the works. One would be perfect for your wedding dinner. I can have a server take the champy to one and also bring you two lovebirds a nice meal."

"That sounds great." Selina realized that she needed to be alone. The gossip had already spread to Janis, which meant that if Selina hung around the bar, she probably wouldn't have a quiet moment to herself away from Marta Hunter and, probably, a lot of other people. "Um, if you see Kam, just point him toward me, okay?"

Taking her champagne flute, Selina followed a server to a foliage-shrouded nook at the farthest end of the beach near the mangrove forest. With a view of the setting sun, but surrounded on three sides by the lavish gardens typical of La Torchere, the bower provided the privacy she needed.

She waited for the server to set up, watching patiently as he put the champagne on ice, brought a glass for Kam and arranged a tray of appetizers. After the server disappeared, she sank down on the sand, ignoring the food and the wine.

She was married, a fate she'd never sought, not since her stepfather had attacked her and she'd developed an aversion to men. Oh, she dated. Danced, touched, kissed. But she'd never had a normal, fulfilled relationship with a man.

And somehow, she'd married the sexy sheik.

"If I ever get my hands on Merry Montrose," she muttered. Did Montrose's employers know the old witch meddled with the love lives of the resort's guests? Well, if they didn't, they sure would after Selina wielded her poison pen. Hunter had nothing on Selina when she had her temper up.

But that wouldn't change anything.

She was married. For good or for evil, richer or poorer, in sickness or in health…as the sun set and the stars emerged, the traditional language rolled through her mind.

Rising, she picked up her champagne flute and regarded the moon, riding high and full in the heavens above. Cold and barren, it seemed a fitting companion for Selina on her loveless, phony wedding night.

She lifted her glass to the moon. "To me." She sipped.

"To my marriage." A bitter laugh broke from her throat.

She refilled her glass and lifted it high. "To love. Whatever that is," she mumbled.

Love. She sat heavily on the sand.

Would she ever know what other women understood? Would she ever fall in love, wear white lace, speak real wedding vows? "Not likely," she murmured, pressing the cool glass against her cheek.

Her work, her friends and her family would have to be enough.

Rebellion rose inside her. Why? Why did she have to be different?

Stop deluding yourself, Selina. You know why.

She remembered what Jerry had said. "If you don't get over it, they win."

She didn't want Donald and Audra to win. That would suck. They didn't deserve to win. They didn't deserve anything.

"I deserve to be happy, dammit," she said aloud, glad she was alone on the beach. She didn't need anyone to see her toasted and morose, but she figured the occasion called for toasted and morose.

She refilled her glass and drank more champagne.

She was married.

Her groom was nowhere in sight.

Nor was anyone else in her family.

She wasn't in love and probably never would be.

Her husband didn't love her and never would.

"Well, life is just a bowl of cherries, and I have found the pits." She gulped champagne, feeling the bubbles inside her throat, scratchy with unshed tears.

Releasing a burp, she giggled, and again was thankful that no one else was on the beach.

How had everything fallen apart? First her father had died. Then Audra had married Donald-the-molester. Then... Selina remembered Donald's hands, scrabbling at her breasts; his breath, heavy with beer, clotting her nostrils.

Despite the night's sultriness, she shivered. Jerry had tried, but it seemed as though nothing could warm the void inside her, empty and chill as the pale moon above.

She was never happy. At best, her most cheerful feelings were…a blank. A big nothing. She felt as though she went through life half-present, with a part of herself, the happy part, lost, gone, forgotten.

She'd forgotten what joy felt like, until this last week.

Kam.

He was a great guy and, dammit, they'd had a chance. Now that frail little chance was blown to smithereens. Thoroughly spooked—and with good reason—he'd get an annulment, and she'd never see him again.

The slight breeze brought her a drift of sound. Music, faint and sweet, from the bar band.

She dropped her glass in the sand and rose, running her hands up her body. The feathers on her dress fluttered against her fingers as she stretched her arms above her, reaching for the moon.

Closing her eyes, she let her body sway to the music of the band, the soft splash of waves caressing the shore.

Then she recognized the tune. "Unforgettable." "No," she whispered, covering her face. She didn't know if she could stand to hear it again. The song was forever tied to her memories of Kam, his seductive kisses, his knowing hands, the warmth in his dark eyes.

Tears rose hot behind her lids, but as she was falling apart, strong arms wrapped around her, holding her together. Without opening her eyes, she sensed Kam's heat, the potency of his embrace, his particular scent that recalled spice and mystery.

His lips touched her closed eyelids, then her cheeks. She knew he'd kissed away her tears. Tasting their saltiness, he chose not to speak of her pain or of anything else, instead holding her close, enveloping her. Warmth grew to heat and then to pleasure, a pleasure heightened by the increasing sensuality of his kisses. He moved from her cheeks to her mouth. She opened to him, seeking the bliss she always found when they kissed.

Her mind stopped, time dissolved, and the world shrank. Nothing existed but Kam's lips on hers, his hands on her body, caressing her into a sensual oblivion.

He slid his fingers into her hair, drawing her head back so he could stroke her throat with his lips. The sensitive skin along her neck loved his mouth, his tongue; every tiny hair on her body prickled in response. Dotting little kisses along his jawline, she pressed her chest against his, seeking the tingling pleasure of her nipples pushing against his solidity.

His hands stroked down to her shoulders, fingers slipping beneath the straps of her dress. She let it drop to her elbows so she could feel her naked breasts against him. She rubbed back and forth, liking the sensation.

But it wasn't enough. She reached for his linen shirt and tugged at the buttons, baring him to the waist.

Though she knew what she'd see, she opened her eyes
to look again.

The muscled planes of Kam's chest were silvered
by the moonlight, the tips of his dark nipples gleaming. On impulse, she laid her palms against them, the
little nubbins hard against the flats of her hands.

He groaned and, with his hands on her hips, slipped
off her dress and eased her down to the sand where
they knelt, facing each other.

She'd never been naked with a man before. A little
embarrassed, she crossed her arms over her chest before deciding she had nothing to be ashamed of. Besides, it was nighttime.

She stared, taking him in: the black hair, with its
subtle waves reflecting the moonlight; eyes dark
pools, mysterious and compelling; smooth, muscled
shoulders and torso. Kam was beautiful, perfectly
formed, the way nature intended a man to look.

He still wore his pants, and she thought, what's fair
is fair, right? She reached for the drawstring.

Selina's eyes were wide, glittering with womanly
knowledge and a purely female readiness Kamar
hadn't yet seen in her. Her skin glowed, damp with
humidity and passion.

Reaching for the drawstring of his pants, she
tugged. They loosened, dropping to his knees. He
heard the quick gasp of her indrawn breath, and he
smiled, knowing he'd pleased her.

He would take what she offered, and give her everything she wanted. He bent his head to her nipples,
feasting on the tight buds, salty and sweet, then

moved to the fragrant hollow between her breasts. Inhaling deeply, he sighed from sheer delight.

She was wonderful, beautiful, better than anyone, even better than his heated dreams of her. The reality of Selina giving herself to him surpassed anything.

He urged her back so she lay flat, then, remembering her past, decided not to crush her beneath his body. Rather, he'd delay his pleasure to give her the release she needed.

But he couldn't resist another kiss from her lush mouth, another nibble on her throat. He slid his tongue down the midline of her body, with quick digressions to her breasts. When he plunged his tongue into her navel, she gasped and giggled, saying her first words of that night, "Don't tease me."

He smiled. "All right." He separated her bent knees. He kissed along her tender white thighs to the feathery curls that hid her female core, then took her with his mouth until she moaned and writhed.

Every cry of joy shot him higher, but he waited for her to lead the way. She reached for him, trying to pull him to her, but he rolled so they lay face-to-face in the yielding sand. She flung one leg over his, giving herself to him. He reached for her bottom, letting his hands sink into the soft rounds until the muscles of her buttocks flexed against his palms.

He brought her closer, so close that he prodded her opening, but still he wouldn't take her. She had to take him, risking that last, ultimate, intimate step.

She did, and when he pressed inside her, he found heaven, a damp, tight nirvana. Selina hadn't lied; her narrowness told him that she hadn't had a lover recently. But he couldn't stop.

He reached between their bodies to caress her, and her gasp dissolved into a throaty moan that spoke of nothing but lust. Wet, she opened to him, admitting him freely. Lips to lips, chest to breast, joined completely with her, he let himself fall into the infinite bliss of Selina's love.

Chapter Fourteen

Chilled to the bone, Selina awoke to see the earliest light of dawn reaching pale fingers across the gray sky. She stretched, feeling sand scratching her back, a new soreness between her legs and Kam's arm across her chest, weighing her down.

Kam...oh, dear Lord, what had she done? She'd had unprotected sex with a man she hardly knew, the fake husband of her phony marriage, a man with an international love-'em-and-leave-'em reputation, a card-carrying Peter Pan par excellence.

She could be pregnant. She could have AIDS. How could she have been so stupid?

She wiggled, trying to squirm out from under his arm without waking him. The last thing she wanted was to have to talk with Kam about what had happened. If she was lucky, she could sneak back to her room without Grandpa Jerry or anyone else being the wiser. Maybe if she didn't talk with Kam, she could pretend that their night on the beach never happened. If he brought it up, she could laugh, tease him about his vivid imagination, and tell him he'd had too much to drink.

Then she'd see a doctor, take a morning-after pill and get checked for STDs. That was the responsible thing to do, wasn't it? And it was about damn time she behaved responsibly.

Okay. First things first... Where was her dress? Turning her head, she spotted it a few feet away.

She slid sideways in its direction, and Kam's arm slid across her chest. His fingers opened, then closed over her breast.

Selina froze in place.

Kam's eyes popped open. "*Ixzit.* What have we done?" He peered at Selina, who pulled away and jumped to her feet.

"Uh, uh...n-nothing really." She backed away.

A viscous liquid dripped along her thigh. Looking down, she saw brown smudges streaking her skin. Mortified, she closed her eyes, though shutting out the world wasn't even a temporary fix.

So much for plan A. Faking that nothing had happened last night was out.

She needed a plan B. Running could work. "Excuse me, please." She reached for her dress, but before she could get it, Kam was on his feet and grabbing her elbow.

"You were a virgin."

She twisted, breaking his grip. "Yeah. So?"

He crossed his arms over his chest. "You could have told me."

"I did tell you." She turned her back to face the ocean. Kam could look at her naked butt, but not the rest of her.

"No, you didn't. You said that you don't sleep around because you had some bad experiences. I assumed that you were celibate, not untouched."

"So don't make assumptions. Besides, what difference should that make?"

"We can't get an annulment."

He still wanted to leave her. A dull ache started beneath her sternum, spreading to encompass her heart. Though surprised, she ignored it. "We can't get an annulment because we had sex, not because I was a virgin."

"We made love," Kam said. "We didn't have sex."

She shrugged. "Call it whatever you want."

"I thought you were an honest woman. Now I understand that you and your grandfather planned this all along, didn't you?"

"What?"

"He proposed this ridiculous engagement idea. Then you led me to city hall. How did you get Hunter to show up and ask about the marriage license?" He grabbed her by the shoulder, jerking her around to face him. "How much did you pay her?"

She batted his hands off her. "How dare you!"

"You've trapped me. Or so you think." He raised his head, jaw tightening. "Zohra-zbel may be a small country, but we have some power. You will not get away with this deception."

"I don't know what you mean," she snapped.

"There was no deception. Look, no one forced you to come down here last night."

"The bartender said you were here," he said. "What was I supposed to do, ignore you on our wedding night? Word would have gotten back to Hunter."

"I should have guessed. Can't you do something nice without an ulterior motive?"

"You're a fine one to accuse me of having ulterior motives."

"No one forced you to have sex with me. I was here, minding my own business—"

"You were crying."

She didn't want to be reminded of her weakness, so she turned away and walked to the shoreline, letting the smallest waves lap at her toes.

"I was concerned for you. When I saw you weeping, I had no thought but to comfort you." He barked out something like a laugh. "I have never before been affected by a woman's tears. They all had seemed contrived, but you…" He shrugged. "You did not know I was watching. Your sorrow was real."

The sea was cool but not uncomfortable. She walked into the water until it was up to her waist, letting the waves wash away the stickiness. The salt tingled in the achy, stretched parts of her body.

She gazed at the gray horizon, resting on the gray ocean, and watched day take over night, with a delicate wash of pink gradually delineating the border between air and water.

The enormity of what she'd done, what they'd done, settled on her like a leaden blanket, weighting her heart. She realized she'd never be the same. She'd given her virginity to her husband on her wedding night, just the way she was supposed to, but everything was as wrong as it could be. Phony husband, fake wedding night, emptiness inside where joy should dwell.

Her sorrow was real, but it was strange that Kam had seen it before she had.

He was behind her again, standing too close, practically breathing down her neck. "When we made love, you were the one to take me."

She didn't turn to face him. She couldn't. The conversation was too intimate. Meeting his eyes would be unbearable, so she continued to stare at the ocean. "I thought it was pretty mutual. We were side by side and it just…happened."

"I had told you that I would wait for you to come to me."

"So you lied." The weight around her heart chilled.

"I told the truth. When we were lying together, you pushed yourself onto me. You took me. I did not take you."

Whirling, she confronted him. "Hey, I've had enough of this I-forced-you jibber-jabber."

He flushed.

"I know what being forced feels like, so just shut up. Just shut up. How dare you?" She shoved a palm into his chest, pushing him away. He fell on his butt into the shallow water with a splash. She stood over him, yelling. "I was a virgin. You've had so many women you've probably lost count. You're the sexy sheik, remember?"

He stood, his jaw tightening even more. He looked as though he was about to explode into a million stressed-out pieces. "You don't understand. How could you? You're a commoner, a nobody. This is a disaster for my country."

"You are a total egomaniac. You're so full of yourself that I'm surprised there's room inside your self-absorbed, arrogant head for worries about anything else, including your country. But I doubt that Zohraz—wherever is going to fall into the sea because we messed up."

"*We* messed up?" His eyes remained bright and accusatory.

"Yeah. *We* messed up. I'm willing to shoulder my share of the blame, but only my share." Pushing past him, she walked out of the sea to her dress. After shaking the sand out of it, she slipped it over her head. "Feel free to file for a divorce. I'll sign whatever papers your attorney sends me. You can contact me through Grandpa Jerry's office."

Chapter Fifteen

Kamar showered and packed, then found Jerome Carrington in The Greenhouse Café finishing breakfast in the company of Emma Forsythe. Carrington's eyes gleamed with interest as he surveyed Kamar. He hoped Selina hadn't talked with her grandfather. If she kept silent, Kamar could avoid discussing the fiasco.

After greeting Carrington and Forsythe, Kamar swallowed, then said, "I must return to my country to take care of some urgent business that has arisen."

"What a shame," Forsythe said. "My daughter has been looking forward to furthering her acquaintance with you."

Kamar guessed that neither Forsythe nor Carrington knew of his marriage to Selina. Otherwise, Mrs. Forsythe would not be so eager to throw Cynthia at him.

"And I, also." Kamar directed his gaze to Jerome. "But I am concerned about our, um, other business."

"Not to worry." Jerry rose. "Please excuse me, my dear. Shall I see you by the pool in, say, an hour?"

Kamar left The Greenhouse, sweating from the hot sun and his proximity to Carrington. Fortunately, Jerome appeared oblivious. "Let's check the business center. The seller should have responded to our offer by now."

When they spoke with the concierge, an attractive older woman, she said, "Oh, yes. A fax did come in last night. There's been some trouble with the fax machine, but we got it straightened out."

"Where is the fax?" Kamar asked.

The concierge took a sheaf of papers out of her desk and handed it to Jerome Carrington, who said, "Let's go to my suite and review this."

Oh, no, Kamar thought. He'd surely see Selina if he went to the Carrington suite, and she was the last person on earth he could face. He could barely look Jerome in the eye after what he'd done, and seeing Selina after the hurtful, wicked things he'd said...Kamar winced.

He'd been a fool, not because she'd tricked him into marriage, but because he'd forgotten everything he knew about Selina. She was the last woman who'd bother entrapping him into marriage. First of all, she truly didn't like him. She'd said over and over again that she considered him arrogant. He thought that perhaps she'd changed her mind about him, but her words that morning showed that she believed he was concerned only with himself. Further, he now understood she wasn't playing at the game of dance-away lover, but her urge to stay unattached was as essential a part of her as her blue eyes. She hadn't planned to get involved with him, but through the machinations of Marta Hunter and Jerome Carrington, she was as stuck as was he in an ugly spiderweb of trickery and deception.

He sighed. What would be the outcome of this game? Kamar didn't know, but he figured he'd have to see it through. He said to Carrington, "Yes, let's go to your suite. I'm…eager to see Selina this morning."

"Oh, she's at the resort spa." Jerome pushed his card key into the elevator's slot. "Didn't she tell you?"

"Um, no."

"She left me a note saying she was sore from the parasailing yesterday and wanted a massage. She got sunburned, so I think she also scheduled a facial."

"Oh." Kamar breathed easier. "I'm sorry I won't see her before I leave. Maybe we can get together when I go to D.C. to take possession of the house."

The elevator opened at their floor, where a bellman loaded Kamar's luggage onto a cart. "I'll be down in a few minutes." He slipped the bellman a five, then followed Jerome Carrington into his suite.

Jerome sat on the couch and began looking through the papers. "How long are you going to be gone?"

Kamar cleared his throat. "I'm not sure."

"Well, the seller accepted your offer."

"He should have. It was a full-price offer in cash."

Jerome smiled, no doubt thinking of his commission. "When do you want to move in?"

* * *

By claiming exhaustion, Selina was able to avoid others for the rest of the day, having contact only with a doctor at the resort's clinic and a masseuse. With Kam paying for their suite, she charged everything to his bill, scheduling massages every day she'd remain at La Torchere.

She longed for the familiar comforts of home, but how could she explain herself to Grandpa Jerry? He'd already purchased plane tickets from Florida to D.C. for the two of them for the following Saturday, one week away. He disliked traveling alone, so she didn't want to let him down, but she wasn't ready to talk about what had happened with Kam. Casual chatter was also beyond her.

The light spa dinner she ate didn't dispel her heavy mood. After the quiet, solitary meal, she phoned the suite. No one answered, so she assumed Jerry was out wooing Emma Forsythe. Selina hadn't liked the woman when they'd met, but right now she blessed Emma and her daughter. They were a welcome distraction for Grandpa Jerry.

But on Sunday afternoon matters came to a head when Jerry burst into Selina's room waving a newspaper.

"*Ixzit,*" she said. "The *Washington Post.* What do they say about me?"

"You and Prince Kamar got married and no one told me!" Jerry slumped onto the edge of her bed and gazed at her reproachfully. "Don't you think I deserve better?"

She sat up and adjusted the terry robe she wore.

"Yes, you do, and if it had meant anything we would have told you."

"Why did he leave so soon?"

"To get a divorce."

"Oh, no! But the two of you were getting along so well."

She rubbed her temple. "Yes, we were, until we got married. I guess…I guess that just happens sometimes."

"Not to you. Not to my girl." He hugged her.

Her heart split in two. "Oh, Grandpa Jerry, everything's just so messed up." Her lips began to tremble. To control herself, she bit down hard, drawing tears.

"What happened?" He hugged her closer.

She tucked her head into the hollow of his shoulder. "What did the paper say?"

"That the two of you eloped, secretly getting a marriage license and executing it. I have to say that it doesn't sound much like you."

She managed a bit of a smile. "No, it doesn't. I never intended to marry."

"Sure you did."

She blinked, easing away from him.

"Look at this." Jerry took his wallet from his back pocket, opened it, and extracted a photo. Worn around the edges, it was evidently one of his treasures. The image was of a little redheaded girl in a voluminous wedding dress, complete with veil and flowers.

"That's me," she said slowly. "I was…about five?"

"Seven." Smiling, Jerry rubbed his finger along the picture's edge. "Wedding day was one of your favorite games. First your dad and mom would tell you about their wedding day, show you the album, and then you'd dress up.''

"I don't remember that at all.''

"I guess it was overshadowed by your dad's death and Audra's, um, peculiar behavior.'' Jerry grimaced.

Selina shoved the subject of her mother out of her mind. "Why didn't you show me this photo before?''

"Just didn't come up, I guess.'' He tucked it back in his wallet before putting an arm around her shoulders. "Don't let Audra and Donald destroy your dreams, honey. You and Prince Kam really liked each other, didn't you?''

Tears flooded her eyes. "Yes, we did,'' she whispered.

"He'll be back,'' Jerry said with certainty.

She shrugged. "Maybe.''

He gazed at her steadily. "If he does, are you going to hide out in your room like you've been doing for the past two days? Is my girl gonna show the white feather?''

She jerked upright. "Heck, no!''

"If he comes back, I want you to give him a chance.''

She pursed her lips. "Maybe.'' She wondered what Kam was doing. Probably getting a divorce while wooing some nubile Zmar-zbel chick…or whatever his country was called. She wished him good luck. Despite what she'd said to Grandpa Jerry, she really didn't want him back.

"You did what?'' Seated at his huge, elaborately carved desk, the king glared at Kamar, who stood at attention before his father. In a nearby doorway, Crown Prince Denya lounged against a lintel, his casual stance belying the seriousness of the conversation.

"Let me understand this correctly," the king continued. "You married a virgin from a good family, despoiled her, then walked out on her. Is that right?"

Kamar stared at his father. Never in his craziest dreams had he imagined the king's reaction. Oh, he'd expected anger, even fury, but not because he'd wronged the woman. "I thought you'd be upset because I can't make a political marriage."

"We had no plans for you, so there's no loss. Besides, one arranged marriage in the family is enough." Denya glanced to a sofa at the side of the room, where Amira, his wife, nursed their third child, a daughter named Sadira.

Amira winked and said, "She must be a clever girl, this American, to have snared you, brother."

"She did not snare me," Kamar said. "She feels as trapped as I do. But she is very clever. She graduated from business school and has a good job in public relations."

"Public relations?" the king asked. "Then she will be an asset to us. PR is diplomacy applied to retail sales. What kinds of products does she sell?"

Kamar frowned at the incongruity of Selina's thoughts issuing from his father's mouth. "Her latest ad campaign was about a cereal, Corny Crunch."

"Horny crunch?" Denya asked in English, laughing while the king and Amira, neither of whom understood the slang, looked confused.

Kamar rolled his eyes. "Oh, like I haven't heard that one a few times before."

Denya grinned and said in Arabic, "I'm sure she's attractive and presentable."

"Beyond attractive. Really quite gorgeous," Kamar said, thinking of Selina's hair, her neck, her eyes, her…her everything.

"You sound very enthusiastic about her, brother." Amira lifted the baby to her shoulder and patted her back. Sadira responded with a hearty burp.

"I guess I am. She really is a great girl," Kamar said.

"Good." The king stood. "Then it's settled."

Kamar stiffened. "What's settled?"

"You're now our ambassador to the United States. Go back and make up with your wife. Good job, Kamar. Your marriage to an American girl will solidify our relationship with them. Now, how about some tea?"

Everyone but Kamar left the room, and he slumped into a chair. Though he had his orders, he didn't know quite how he felt about them. Was he ready for the responsibility of a wife? Not judging by the way he'd treated his! Selina was a terrific person, but he'd treated her so badly, he didn't know if he could win her love.

However, he knew he'd better obey his father.

He wondered what Selina was doing. In her newly vulnerable state, could another man be horning in on his wife? A female who was nursing disappointment was easy prey for a wolf. Many women had sought his comfort after an affair gone wrong, so he was in a special position to divine the intentions of other males. He used to be the other man, the wolf stalking easy female prey.

He figured he'd better get back to Florida. Fast.

Chapter Sixteen

On Tuesday afternoon, Selina encountered the resort manager outside the spa. "Ms. Montrose," she said frigidly. "Do you know what you've done?"

The older woman's hands worked. "I don't know what you mean."

"Don't lie to me." Selina advanced on her. "You married Kam Asad and me without our knowledge or consent, and now he's gone."

"Oh, no!" Montrose put a hand to her mouth.

"Oh, yes. He's gone to get us a divorce."

Montrose looked stricken.

"And you know what? Kam and I liked each other. We might have had a chance. But you just had to meddle, didn't you? You and that witch Marta Hunter—"

"Hunter's not a witch," Montrose said.

Selina ignored her. The tears she'd held back for days flooded her eyes, and her voice dropped to a whisper. "We had a chance, but now he's gone. And it's your fault."

Whirling, Montrose fled. A mean part of Selina was glad that she'd made someone else feel as lousy as she did.

After her massage, she dressed in the same pair of denim shorts and T-shirt she'd worn for the past two days. She planned to eat a light dinner back at her suite while finishing the latest volume of the Harry Potter books. Bliss!

But there *he* was, like the proverbial bad penny: Kam Asad, her sort-of husband, a man she never expected to see again. Wearing his usual loose white linen, he leaned casually against her doorway as though he hadn't a care in the world. The wretch.

Every muscle in her body tightened into steel cables, trashing three days of relaxing massages. She felt like Harry confronting Voldemort, with the same mixture of hope, desperation and fear.

She'd missed Kam. She wanted what her husband could give her, but the reality of Kam and what he'd said warred with her hopes, her dreams and her memories of the fun times they'd had.

Plus, there was the potential their friendship—she wouldn't call it a romance or a relationship—had once shown. She'd meant what she'd told Merry Montrose. She and Kam had once had a chance, but it was gone.

She'd thought it was over between them, but here he was. What could he want?

Though anxious, Selina wouldn't back down. Closing in on him, she tamped down her hope and focused instead on her anger. "So, it's you," she snapped. "What do you want?"

He pushed away from the lintel, smiling, and held out his hands. "You, of course."

She gave him a brief, contemptuous laugh. "Please tell me you're joking." Avoiding his embrace, she shoved the card key into the lock, opened the door and walked past him into the suite.

He followed. She had to admire his gall while loathing the rest of him.

"What are you doing in here?" she asked.

"Talking to you."

"Not anymore. Door's that way. Out." She pointed.

"I'm not leaving until you listen to what I have to say."

"What for? I heard everything you had to say on Sunday morning, thank you very much."

He winced. "I apologize. I said many things that weren't true. Hurtful things that you didn't deserve."

She stopped, startled. "Kam Asad apologizing? The prince of Zorah-z-whatever admitting he was wrong? Wow. This must be a historic occasion. Maybe I should call Marta Hunter so she can get the scoop."

He ignored her sarcasm. "Has she still been bothering you?"

"No, because I haven't been out and about very much."

"Why not?"

She put a hand on her hip. "Well, it's just a little embarrassing for the entire world to know that I got married but that my husband walked out on me the very next day.''

"That was also a mistake. I should have taken you with me.''

"Excuse me? What makes you think I would have gone anywhere with you?''

"Oh, you would have. After that night, I could have taken you anywhere.'' He gave her that slow, sexy, intimate smile again, the one he'd probably practiced in front of a mirror when he was a teenager.

But it got to her anyhow. She was becoming all itchy and twitchy again, tingly in all the places where he'd first awakened tingles, out on the beach under the moonlight.

She ignored the tingles and concentrated instead on his massive arrogance and his mean temper. "You probably shouldn't bring up that night.''

"Why not? It was wonderful.''

"Unfortunately, you're not nearly as wonderful in the morning. You know, you're a real son-of-a-gun until you have your morning cup of tea.'' She crossed her arms over her torso.

"How many times do I have to apologize for what I said?''

"You don't have to apologize at all. You can leave. I don't have anything to say to you, and I'm not interested in what you have to say to me.''

"I am your husband and I ask that you listen to me, trust me.''

"Trust you? You're not my husband. You're a guy I married by mistake.''

"We made love and it mattered.''

"Did it?" Her lip curled. "Sure couldn't tell by your reaction. You grabbed me, yelled at me, accused me of horrible, dishonest things, and then you left. You went thousands of miles away. How great could the sex have been for you? Heck, you could hardly wait to leave, and then you went half a world away." To her shame and embarrassment, the damn tears started again. She turned away so he couldn't see them. He didn't deserve any part of her, and certainly not her tears.

He touched her shoulder, making everything worse. "Don't pretend, and don't change the subject. It mattered to me, which was why I said those terrible things. It mattered so much that I was bad to you, my wife. It mattered to me and it had to matter to you. It was your first time." His voice was gentle.

Her lips compressed. She leaned her forehead against the wall, feeling it cool on her heated skin. "More's the pity."

"Did you wish to remain a virgin forever?" He moved in closer to her, crowding her with his big body. "The way you kiss, I'm surprised you stayed inviolate so long."

She lifted her chin. "I had my reasons."

"You had one reason, and it doesn't exist."

"You just don't get it, but there's no reason why you should." That tiredness, that lead blanket weighing her down, returned again, draping itself heavily over her heart.

"Your reason is in the past—eight years in the past!"

She turned and shook her head slowly. "Kam,

you're not like me. You've been spoiled all your life. On top of that, you don't know anything about women. You think you do, but you don't. How could you? The only women you've ever known were servants or throwaway lovers.''

''I know this. But you—you're living in the past, Selina. You have made what happened when you were fifteen your reason for everything, everything you do. The past doesn't exist, Selina. The past is a memory. The future is only a dream. There is only now. You and me, here, now.''

She opened her mouth, then closed it, visibly hesitant. ''Maybe there's some truth in what you're saying. I'm willing to think about it.''

He pressed his body, and his point, closer. ''Do you want to have a life? Then stay with me. Give us a chance. Or you can go back to your Corny Crunch and your empty little job.''

Her eyes chilled from lagoon to iceberg in an instant, and he realized that criticizing her job was a mistake. She said, ''I'm not quitting work, whatever happens.''

Whatever happens. She'd left a chink, a tiny gap through which hope could wriggle. ''Fine,'' he said, immensely relieved. ''But live with me.''

''No. It'll never work out. We're too different!''

''You're a woman and I'm a man. Of course we're different.''

''There are significant cultural differences.''

He shook his head. ''I cannot agree. Before that idiotic marriage, I thought we got along quite well.''

''Ye-es, we did.''

"We had fun, didn't we?"

"Well, yeah!"

"All I'm asking is to have fun with you forever. Is that so bad?"

"See what I mean? We're too different. For you, life is all fun. For me, life is work."

He shrugged. "My work is fun. Isn't yours?"

"Sometimes," she said slowly, sounding thoughtful. "I like the people I work with. I like the creative aspects of producing a marketing campaign. And I really like getting paid."

"So…shall we not try? I understand it will be a big step, for you to close your apartment in D.C. and move into the ambassador's house."

She bit her lip. "Moving is always annoying."

"Yes, it is, but when one has money, one hires people to help."

"I'm not ready for that yet."

"All right. Before taking that radical a step, I propose an experiment."

"What kind of experiment?" she asked warily.

"Let's play house."

"Play house? How and where?"

"Here, at La Torchere, they have little houses. Villas, they call them."

"Pretend to—"

"Yes. You have a few more days of vacation, do you not?"

"Ye-es. I don't have to leave until Saturday."

"All right, then." With a sense of relief, he went to the phone. At last he'd wrested a concession from

Selina. He had a chance. "I shall call the front desk and make arrangements to rent one of the villas."

"Wait!" She put her hand on the phone, stopping him. "How many bedrooms? Two, right? One for you and one for me?"

He examined her, smiling. Her face was flushed, her eyes bright. She wants me, he thought. She wants me so much she's terrified of getting too close. That is my fault, of course, and I will have to work hard to get her back.

But he was willing to put in the time, not because the king, his father, had demanded it, but because Selina Carrington was worth it. He said, "We do not need more than one bedroom."

She crossed her arms over her chest in a closed stance. "I'm not comfortable sleeping with you."

"You seemed most pleased the other night." He tried to sound mild and modest rather than arrogant. Selina did not like his arrogance.

"I was insane the other night."

"Yes, insanely sexy."

She went pink.

He smiled. "Let us compromise. I'll sleep on the couch one night, and after that, we'll see."

She still looked hesitant. One hand went to her mouth, and she bit the knuckle.

He reached for her. "You have continued to wear your ring."

The pink flags in her cheeks deepened to a fetching shade of rose. "I like my ring." She raised it to look into the glowing depths of the ruby, then dropped her hand, as though gazing into the fire too long would burn.

"Your ring symbolizes commitment."

"That wasn't why you bought it for me. You bought it for me as part of that stupid act we put on."

"No. I had wanted to buy you a gift, and when a man gives a woman a ring, it means only one thing. No matter what excuses they may make, no matter what silly things they may say, it means only one thing."

"Huh." She turned that over inside her mind.

"Shall we now go and rent a villa?"

Selina hesitated, then decided that, if necessary, she could retreat to her suite. She wouldn't be trapped.

Besides, she had to admit to herself she had a job that paid peanuts and occupied only a tiny corner of her mind. Most of the time she was bored.

Since she'd met Kam, she'd never been bored. Exasperated, yes. Angered, definitely. Astounded, often. Brought to the heights of ecstasy—yep, that too, tempered by the darkest sorrow and bleakest desolation she'd ever known.

But never bored.

Life with Kam would be exasperating, exciting, challenging...but never dull.

Should she take the chance? Could she survive if it didn't work out?

And what if it did?

"Okay, let's try it." She winked at him. "Just for kicks and giggles."

Chapter Seventeen

Lacking a suitcase, Selina had to borrow one of Kam's, which felt strange but strengthened her sense of intimacy. Sharing personal items did that, she realized, as she gathered together the meager possessions she'd amassed while at La Torchere. She shoved her toiletries into a leather case already partially filled with her husband's razors and combs. She folded her bathing suit into the valise with Kam's shorts and polo shirts. She left her dresses on their hangers so they wouldn't become creased and wore her favorite clunky white platform sandals.

Packing didn't take long, and at sunset she and Kam walked across La Torchere's manicured gardens and along the beach to the villas.

Square white structures covered with stucco, the villas were really more like cottages. Extremely nice cottages. As they entered, she could see that they were fully appointed little houses, with a cozy living room and a kitchen downstairs, and a big bedroom upstairs. The place was decorated in inoffensive shades of oatmeal and white, with touches of color from plants, flowers and a bowl of fruit that the staff had left on the kitchen counter.

Two bathrooms tiled in white were conveniently located on each floor. The one downstairs had a stall shower. Selina didn't like to share her bathroom, and she let Kam know that right away by unpacking her toiletries in the upstairs bath and arranging his toiletries downstairs.

"What's this?" he asked, picking up one of his hairbrushes.

"A hairbrush, I guess." Wooden-handled, it had what she thought were black boar bristles on the operative side.

"That's not what I meant. Why is it here? Where are yours?"

"In the upstairs bathroom."

He frowned. "That was not the deal. We are supposed to live as man and wife."

She eyed him. "Honey, we could live as *husband* and wife for twenty years, but I still wouldn't share a bathroom with you. I never even shared a bathroom with Grandpa Jerry."

"And you call me spoiled," he grumbled. "What did you do at college?"

"Worked, so I could afford my own apartment with my own bathroom. I can't help it, I'm picky. Who wants your nose hairs in the sink?"

He reared back, visibly affronted. "I do not leave nose hairs in the sink."

She gave him her sweetest smile. "Maybe there's hope for this marriage after all."

"And this couch…" He ambled out of the bathroom to the villa's living room, where a comfortable-looking couch occupied the wall facing an entertainment center. He lay on it and stretched. His feet hung over one end. "It's too short. I won't sleep even a wink. Are you sure—"

"Yes, I'm sure. Scoot off for a second."

He scooted, and she moved cushions around to discover that the couch folded out into a queen-size bed. "Perfect."

"All right," he said grudgingly. "Now how about supper and a walk along the beach?"

"Okay. Do you want to go fancy or casual?"

"Let's dress, I think. I'd like to see you in that beautiful white dress you wore for our first dinner."

"Can't think of a reason why not." She went to change.

A half hour later, they walked hand in hand toward the center of La Torchere. "How about The Greenhouse Café?" Kam asked. "We've never tried dinner there."

The Greenhouse was magical at night, with tiny fairy lights illuminating the cavernous space. Inside, it was cooler than during the day, and Kam draped his arm over her bare shoulders as they walked over the bridge.

For supper, The Greenhouse served bistro-style fare. After they'd eaten chicken with a nice Chardonnay, they strolled along the moonlit beach, with Selina feeling pleasantly full and relaxed.

"So far, so good," she said to Kam. "Maybe I can do this marriage thing." Her platforms sank into the sand, and she stopped to slip them off.

He took them from her and stuck his fingers through the back straps, letting them dangle from his hands as they walked. "Of course you can. Millions of people have very happy marriages. Why shouldn't we?"

"Well, we started off kind of...funny."

"Strange funny, not ha-ha funny, right?"

"Yeah." As they passed the bar, she could hear the band playing a rowdy rendition of "Twist and Shout" with a karaoke singer butchering the rock and roll classic.

"It would be less strange if we slept together, my wife," Kam said.

"Oh, quit harping on that." But she couldn't put any sting into her words; she felt too good. "Let's dance instead."

"I do not think it would be seemly for a prince of Zohra-zbel to twist and shout." He grinned.

"That's just an excuse."

He chuckled. "Yes, it is." His cell phone rang, and he answered it.

Disappointment stabbed. Would she ever have her husband to herself? Would Kam's phone fixation ever cease? She was conscientious about her job, but he took workaholism to an extreme. With a sigh, she reminded herself that his work wasn't like hers. He'd been born into his job, and it was one that couldn't be avoided or shirked.

They'd reached the villa, and, without missing a

word of his conversation, Kam opened the door for her. Fighting tears, she headed for the staircase and her bed.

He closed the phone and intercepted her before she placed even one foot on a riser. "I'd like a good-night kiss, please," he said.

A warm tide of affection rose in her chest. He cared, after all. Maybe a little. Otherwise, his motivation was obscure to her. Despite his insistence on remaining married, he hadn't said a word of love but had only talked about having fun.

She wasn't sure that fun was enough, but she had to admit she'd never found anything lacking in his kisses—and tonight's good-night kiss was no exception.

She didn't want to mislead him or become tempted to rush their romance, so she broke it off before they got into the kiss too deeply. "I'd better get to bed," she said, keeping her tone casual.

But moving in with Kam hadn't felt casual. Oh, she'd faked it well, she thought, but it was weird, lying alone in a big king-size bed, listening to the sound of the TV as he watched Letterman before he switched off his light. Then she heard every creak as he rolled around in his foldout bed downstairs before the villa went silent.

She stared at the ceiling and longed for rest. Hours later, she turned her head to see that the digital clock by her bedside registered three-fifteen. The villa was silent, and she resented Kam's ability to fall asleep when she couldn't. She finally fell into a restless slumber sometime before dawn.

When she awakened, her nose twitched at the heavenly scent of coffee. Thoughtful of Kam to have ordered room service early, she thought as she washed her face and scrambled into her clothes. She hurried to the villa's little kitchen to find Kam, naked to the waist, pouring coffee, brewing tea and arranging croissants on a flowered plate, his dark face intent on his culinary tasks.

She stopped. She hadn't seen his bare flesh since their fateful encounter on the beach, and even then, his body had been silvered by moonlight and shadowed by the night. Now, his golden skin gleamed in the morning sunlight streaming through the villa's windows. She might not have a perfect relationship with her husband, but she couldn't deny his attractiveness or obvious virility.

Swallowing, she approached, deciding to crack a joke, toss out a witty quip—her usual defense mechanism. But words failed her. The memories were too overwhelming, her neediness too extreme.

"Hi," she managed to say.

He raised his gaze to her, and the darkness of his visage was broken by a brilliant smile. "Good morning, my wife." Coming to her, he took her in his arms and kissed her soundly, his embrace warm and possessive. "But what is this?" He fingered the lapel of her jacket.

"It's a business suit." She'd arrived wearing it.

He drew away. "I know that. I'm not stupid. Why are you wearing it?"

"Aren't we pretending this is a normal life? I thought that, um, if it was an ordinary workday I'd dress the part." She couldn't resist another glance at his chest. "I guess you thought differently."

"I did bring a suit, but it is not appropriate for the Florida weather." He gave her a frown. Not a mean frown but a confused and thoughtful one. "There is such a thing as too much pretense, you know. If we go to lunch, I would not want to draw attention."

"But this is what I would normally wear."

"There is nothing normal about the situation."

"Really? I hadn't noticed." To take the edge off her words, she said, "Coffee and croissants. You... you remembered what I eat for breakfast."

"Of course. You are my wife. I am quite aware of your needs and *very* ready to satisfy them." He went to the refrigerator. When he opened it, she could see that it was stacked with food. He took out two fruit compotes, artfully arranged in cut-crystal bowls, and set them on the counter.

Kam intended to cook for her.

Since her childhood, no one in her life had nurtured her in this way. Not even Grandpa Jerry fixed meals for her; he left that to his housekeeper.

Once again words failed her, so she fell back on manners. Thank heaven for manners. Without them she'd be adrift on a sea of silent ineptitude.

"Thank you." She sat on one of the bar stools at the counter.

They ate, and after breakfast, Kam got his briefcase and set to work, wondering what Selina would do with herself. Wasn't she on vacation?

She flipped open a laptop and started to answer e-mails while he found the floor plan of the house he'd just purchased, the ambassador's residence in Washington, D.C. He figured that if he was going to live there, it should be remodeled to his specifications.

After opening the roll of paper, he stretched it over the kitchen table and anchored its corners with salt shakers, sugar bowls and his coffee mug. Contemplating the lobby, he began to make sketches and lists of materials.

A few minutes later she asked, "What are you doing?"

He stretched his arms above his head, deliberately showing off his body to his wife. Her eyes tracked his every movement, and he smiled. With luck, he'd bed her tonight, and there would be no more silly talk about divorcing.

His family would be happy, Selina would be *very* happy, and as for Kam himself…well, he'd known that he'd have to marry one day, so what was the difference?

His father was right. Selina was a nice girl from a good family. He'd been lucky to find a sweet, sexy American woman with a beautiful neck who was well educated and a virgin to boot.

Given what she had been through, she was truly quite amazing. He'd meant what he'd told his family. Selina was a terrific girl. He'd try to be open to loving her; she deserved that. She'd be a fine ambassador's wife, and they'd have many good times together.

He said, "I'm planning the foyer of the ambassador's residence in D.C."

"Don't you like what's already there?"

"It is not grand enough. I want marble and pillars."

"Are you crazy? Who wants to live with marble and pillars?"

Belatedly, Kam remembered that Selina would be living there, also. "What do you think?"

"I think you're going about this the wrong way. We're talking about a home, Kam, the place where we'll live. Where our—" She stopped her quick mouth before she said, "Where our children will grow up."

"Where our what?"

"Where our friends will visit. Why do you want to make it a cold, marble-clad showplace?"

"I want it to impress."

"Intimidate."

He stroked his chin. Selina couldn't help noticing his strong, smoothly shaven jawline. She recalled dotting kisses along his jawline on their wedding night.

She ignored her memories and said, "Arrogant and pretentious." She wagged her head with mock sorrow. "Have I taught you nothing?"

"I think I am being very nice to you."

She smiled. "You are."

He edged closer to her. "And I want to be even nicer."

"But you have to think about being nice to visitors, don't you?"

He looked baffled.

"Diplomacy is PR, remember? PR is all about being nice. Approachable. Friendly. Pillars and marble aren't friendly. They're the exact opposite of friendly."

"Hmm." Perhaps she was right. His father had also

seen the connection between Selina's work and the business of foreign relations. "What do you suggest?" he asked.

"The embassy can be the impressive showplace," she said. "Let's make this house a home, okay?"

Chapter Eighteen

"If we take it room by room, we can both have what we want." Later that day Kam paced restlessly back and forth through the small living room.

She followed, wondering if he would wear a trail in the beige Berber carpet. "But the house will benefit from a unified color scheme. A plan. That way each room will flow into the next. I don't want the house to look patchworky."

"Boring, the pale colors you want."

She'd been pushing for pastel peach and cream with teal accents. "Unified."

"Dull, like this place." Kam waved a hand. "Everything is the same. No soul."

"If we go for the maroon and forest-green that you want, not only will the house be dark, but it will look like Christmas year-round. Yuck."

"Strong, solid, masculine colors." He winked at her.

"Maybe we should hire a decorator to help."

"I don't want my house to look as though a decorator did it."

"It won't, after we—it starts getting lived in." She'd almost slipped again, implying they'd live together when she really hadn't decided.

He smirked at her. The glint in his eye told her that the slip hadn't gone unnoticed. "Especially if we have children."

Jolted, she said, "Children? What about children? Who said anything about children?"

"We might have some. You know, Selina, you may already be pregnant."

"I'm not. I went to a doctor to make sure."

"You did? That was very smart."

"You're not upset?" She examined him, but his facial expression remained calm and open, tinctured with a little good humor.

"No. I have made sure I never sired a child. I don't believe in out-of-wedlock babies. Bad for the family."

"Oh." She hadn't known before that Kam, who looked and acted as though he was a Peter Pan to the core, had any interest in healthy families. She certainly hadn't any inkling that he wanted one for himself. But she supposed he'd have to, wouldn't he? He was a prince, and a main interest of royals was continuing their line.

With her aversion to men, she had figured that children would never be a part of her future. If she stayed with Kam, she'd have to change her plans. She didn't know how she felt about that.

"But babies in general—" He spread out his hands.

His long strong fingers reminded her of their love-making, and how his hands had roamed her body, pleasuring her.

Ixzit. Here was that itchy, twitchy, needy feeling again. She suppressed it, but with more difficulty than before.

"I am in favor of babies," he continued. "If two people are married, babies naturally follow most of the time."

"Th-that's true."

"Are you?"

"Am I what?"

"In favor of babies."

"I'm...I'm not sure."

"Best decide soon." He smiled into her eyes, his intentions blatant. He meant to bed her, and soon.

Did he also intend to get her pregnant? Then she couldn't easily escape their marriage. But now, with the two of them getting along so well, she didn't know if she wanted to escape.

Besides, there was that itchy, twitchy need, grown big, constant and overwhelming, impossible to ignore. She fumbled for an answer. "Uh, okay."

Was she ready for another intimate encounter with Kam? She'd enjoyed the first one, but the aftermath had been hell.

That night they ate at their villa, with Kam barbecuing lamb outside on a little hibachi they'd found in a storage space. "This is the way we cook in Zohrazbel," he told her, rubbing a spice mixture between his palms, then sifting the powders onto the sizzling skewers of meat. "Even in the palace, we will often light a fire in a courtyard and cook out in the open air. It is better so."

Selina sniffed, the aromas reminding her of Kam's distinctive, exotic scent. "What did you eat in England, when you went to school?"

He frowned, turning the skewers. "The dinners offered at school were execrable. I survived mostly on high tea and pub food. I ate a lot of finger sandwiches, grilled salmon, fish and chips, that sort of thing."

"And beer."

"Yes, beer. The British brew excellent beer. I shall have to take you to Cambridge," he said in his precise accent. "And to my homeland, of course. Everyone is quite eager to meet you."

"They are?"

"Yes." He smiled at her. "Despite what you may have heard about other royal families, ours is quite close."

After they finished their meal with dessert and coffee, they walked, this time toward the dark, mysterious mangrove forest. At the water's edge, the roots of the big, weirdly shaped trees plunged directly into the surf, so Kamar guided Selina inland, finding a path through the darkness. Little moonlight pierced the canopy of thick leaves and branches above them. After a few paces in, he took her elbow to lead her down the trail.

"Do you have good night vision?" she asked. "I can't see a thing."

Curious, he thought. He could see their path with ease. "Yes, I think so. I was not raised in a city, you see. My country is not heavily industrialized, so the nights are not brightly lit. I suppose because of that, my night vision remains well exercised and sharp.''

''That's a theory, I guess.'' She sounded dubious.

''As you Americans would say, that's my story and I'm sticking to it.''

She giggled, a girlish, appealing sound, and he swung her around to plant a kiss on her open, laughing mouth. She continued to smile as they kissed and touched, and his heart jumped a little.

Progress was being made. They'd had a perfect day, with the both of them collaborating on a very personal project: their home. Should he broach the subjects of their bedroom and the children's nursery on the morrow?

Perhaps. But now they had the night, and everything he wanted to happen in the next few hours was so much more important than the color scheme of the master bath.

Selina was a smart woman. She'd shown time and again that he couldn't deceive or bamboozle her. He didn't know how to win her except through his love, and the only way he knew how to show her his love was physically, through lovemaking.

She deserved his best, and he would give that to her.

When they reached their villa, he began to kiss her more deeply. She didn't resist; why should she? She'd always enjoyed kissing Kam. The physical part of their relationship had never been a problem.

''Mmm...'' She let herself sink into Kam's embrace, let him caress her lips with his, opened to him willingly. Followed his lead when he opened the door and eased her over to the couch. Let him press her down into the cushions.

Let him cover her body with his.

She'd thought that his weight would frighten her, but it didn't. He didn't feel like Donald, smell like Donald or taste like Donald. He wasn't ripping at her clothes or forcing her the way Donald had.

Kam smelled and felt like Kam. Intimacy with her husband was an utterly distinctive sensual experience. She could never confuse him with anyone else. He tasted pleasantly of the crème brûlée they'd shared for dessert, with a lovely bitter undertone of espresso.

She couldn't get enough of him, and found herself twining around him like a vine on a tree, with the heat in her body rising to match his.

He broke away and whispered in her ear, his voice husky, "Do you wish to stay with me tonight, my wife?"

"I'm not sure," she whispered back.

He feathered his lips along her neck, and she moaned. With an effort she controlled herself. "I just don't want to mess up anything by rushing."

He stopped. "You are right. We rushed before, and look what happened."

"I know. I don't want to mess up again. We have a chance, Kam, and I—"

"I know." He placed a finger on her lips, and she opened her mouth and licked the tip. He groaned. "Stop that."

He pressed his hips into hers, and his desire nudged, long and hard, at her most sensitive places.

She wiggled back and forth, rubbing him once, twice, three times. With each push, a jolt of pleasure rushed through her. Need tugged at her, insistent and demanding.

Kam's sharply indrawn breath told her that she'd gotten to him. "You must make a choice," he whispered. "If you will stop, stop now."

"Maybe I don't want to stop."

"Be sure."

"I'm sure. Are you? I don't want to be accused again of forcing you." She grinned at him so he would know she was teasing.

He smiled back. She was delighted that he understood. She had a husband with a sense of humor.

"I want to make love to you," he whispered. "Very much."

She swallowed and said, "Yes."

She led him upstairs, to the bed that had seemed so broad and cold and empty the night before with only her slender body to fill it. Now Kam dominated the wide, white sheets, his body gleaming in the moonlight that streamed in through the open curtains.

She'd worn shorts for their informal meal, and he made quick work of them, tugging the elastic waist down over her hips while she pulled her T-shirt over her head. His mouth found her breast, and she moaned, pulling him closer.

She remembered from the last time, the first time, that blessed sense of completion she'd never before felt. She had to have it again, craved it with a clawing, desperate need she couldn't, and didn't want to, control.

A part of her prayed that tomorrow morning
wouldn't be a disaster, and then Kam's mouth traveled lower, seeking her delta, and she forgot how to
think, forgot everything except the insistent push of
his tongue against her.

Chapter Nineteen

Two days later, on Friday morning, Selina awakened to a brilliant, sunshiny day, with golden light streaming in through the curtains. Beside her Kam slept, breathing deeply but not, thank the heavens, snoring. She didn't know if she could tolerate a snoring husband.

She stretched, grabbing the headboard with her fingers while touching the bottom edge of the bed with her toes. A divine sense of well-being enveloped her; if she didn't hold the headboard, she might float away.

How everything had changed! Two weeks ago she hadn't met Kam, hadn't an inkling that life could feel so good, that *she* could feel so good. And the best part of it was that she'd learned how to make someone else feel good, too.

Oh, not in the distant, fake way she always had. She'd been controlled and polite. But now she realized that her courtesy hadn't stemmed from fondness toward others. Before Kam, she'd always kept people at arm's length. Now she understood her deep need to give and to receive affection. Not mere friendliness but love.

He'd changed, as well, or maybe her perception of him had broadened. He'd catered to her needs for days, brewing her coffee in the mornings though he drank tea, noting her preferences in everything. His lovemaking had been tender and unselfish.

He'd lost the arrogance she despised. Though she admitted to herself it was more likely that with her instinctive aversion to men, she'd seen what she'd expected to see when they'd met, overlooking the essentials of Kam's character. She now understood that he was a loving, caring man with a deep capacity to cherish the ones he loved.

He'd freely given her everything he had to give, and in so doing, had won her heart. Having known the joy of living with Kam, she couldn't bear the thought of going back to her empty apartment and sterile future.

They would have a great life together, and she wanted to start that great life now. Nudging him with her elbow, she said, "Wake up, sleepyhead."

Rolling over, he rumbled, bear-like. "Why?"

"It's late. I'm hungry. Aren't you?"

He reached for her. "Hungry for you, my goddess." He ran his fingers lightly along her side, tickling.

She giggled. "Not now. I'm a little sore."

He sat up. "I hurt you. Oh, darling, I'm so sorry."

She hastened to say, "It's okay. We've just been, um, a little active lately. My body's not used to it."

He rubbed his face in her hair. "When will you get used to it?"

"I hope I never take you for granted." She beamed at him. "Just to prove it, let me take you out to breakfast."

She chose The Greenhouse Café, though Kam hadn't been entirely happy about the service when they'd eaten breakfast there before. The server hadn't been able to chase away Marta Hunter, and Selina looked around the crowded tables. No Hunter this time. Relieved, she sighed.

Kam seemed unaware of her concern, seating her, then taking a chair. He unloaded two newspapers and his cell phone, the same way he always did in the morning, then ordered his usual breakfast with the calm affability that she now believed was his usual state. He offered her part of the *Washington Post,* and they chatted amiably about the news of the day until their food arrived.

Then he said, "I understand you return to D.C. on the morrow."

Her throat parched to a desert dryness. She'd guessed that this conversation would take place, but didn't know what to say or how to say it. Picking up her water glass, she sipped to delay the moment of truth.

"Yes," she finally said. "Grandpa Jerry has the tickets. I'm...I'm not quite sure when we're supposed to leave."

Kam leaned back into his chair and regarded her,

his dark eyes unfathomable. "Early, I should think. You must catch the ferry, then go to the airport, pass through security and so forth."

"Yes." She compressed her lips. To deflect him she asked, "What are you going to do?"

He spread out his hands, stretching his long, dark fingers. "I am going to go to Washington, D.C., and live with my wife in the beautiful home we will decorate together."

She drew a breath, feeling it flow through her, grounding her. She said, "You say that as though it's all decided, as though you own me."

"Own you? That is the most ludicrous thought." He leaned over the table toward her, dropping his voice. "It is you who possesses me. You are my goddess. You take me in, surround me, overwhelm me—you have become everything to me."

His dark gaze bored into hers, intense and compelling. "I am not sure how it happened, but it did. I am yours, only yours, forever."

The warmth of his affection enfolded her like an embrace. She reached for his hand, ecstatic. This was *it*. This was what she'd needed, what she'd been praying for, the security and love she'd craved all her life. "Say it," she whispered. "I...I have to hear it. Please."

He smiled and lifted her hand to kiss her fingers. At that moment his cell phone rang. Every one of Selina's muscles tensed. Her temper flared. Annoyance flitted over Kam's face, but he released her, flipped open the phone and answered in Arabic.

She stood. "Excuse me." She took the phone from

his grasp and said into it, "He can't talk now." Then she pitched the phone to the top of The Greenhouse waterfall.

It banged against a high rock ledge before clattering down the length of the fall. Other diners near their table applauded. "Nice pass, lady," one shouted. "You should try out for the Raiders!"

She bowed. "Thank you." She then sat down and grinned at Kam.

He leaned his chin into his hand, smiling. "That was my father."

"Oh, my God." She slapped her palm to her face. She'd probably offended her new father-in-law, a king, no less. "We'd better call him back right away. I have to apologize." She fumbled in her purse for her cell phone. She hadn't carried her purse the entire time she'd been at La Torchere, charging everything to her room. She had it today only because she planned to pay for their meal in cash. "Here, dial him up." She handed her phone to Kam.

Chuckling, he obeyed, while a nearby diner said, "You're kidding me."

She turned. "Hey, it's an emergency."

"They all say that," he grumbled, picking up a slice of bacon.

After a minute or two Kam connected, speaking in rapid Arabic before handing the phone to Selina. "Um, hello, sir," she said cautiously into the phone. How did one address a king? She hadn't a clue. Would he want her to call him Your Majesty? She hoped not. That would be weird.

"Hello, my daughter." The king's voice was rich

and warm, with a delightful accent. He sounded as though he spoke English infrequently.

"Uh, hi. Sorry about that. We were, uh, talking."

"Yes, and I am sorry to have interrupted you. We are delighted to hear that you and Kamar are getting on so well. When will we meet you?"

"I don't know. We're talking about staying together, though."

"It would give us much pleasure if you would remain with my son," the king said. "He needs the steadying influence of marriage to a nice girl."

Selina's mind whirled.

"When he came to visit us last week and told us of you, I thought you sounded perfect." The king couldn't have seemed kinder, but Selina's heart chilled, as though an icy blanket of suspicion encased it, freezing her joy.

"Is that right?"

"Oh, yes. I was appalled at how he had treated you. I have told him time and again that he had to manage his women more honorably."

Manage his women. Could this conversation get any more horrible? But she had to know. "What, exactly, did you tell him?" She eyed Kam.

"That he had to go back to America and make it up to you."

"Oh."

Realization struck Selina like the devil's hammer.

Kam hadn't come back to her of his own free will.

He'd seduced her into loving him, but not because he loved her. He'd been following orders.

Her hand holding the cell phone began to quiver.

She clenched the phone, ruthlessly quenching her shakes. Her insides began to churn with fury, covering her deep hurt. You will not cry, she commanded herself. Whatever happens, you will not cry in public.

"And now everything is all right, yes?" The king was incongruously cheerful, without a clue that he'd just destroyed her world.

She swallowed and pressed her lips together. "I'm not sure that I would use the phrase *all right*. Certainly I am now in a position to make the correct decision." She glared at Kam, whose brows had drawn together. The snake.

Kamar's heart sank. What on earth had his father said? As she'd talked, Selina's mood had visibly altered. Her smile had been replaced by a frown. No, a grimace. Her very posture had stiffened. His beautiful, sexy goddess of a wife, the woman he'd fallen for, had been replaced by the snappish young chit he'd met in the bar less than two weeks before.

"Thank you, sir," Selina said into the phone, her tone formal. "Do you want to speak with Kamar again?" She handed the phone across the table.

Kamar took the phone and hastily concluded the conversation while watching Selina stand, open her purse and extract money. She tossed it onto the table with a defiant flip of her hand, then took off her ruby ring. After she dropped it into his teacup with a decisive splash, she walked out, leaving him.

Chapter Twenty

After fumbling for her ring in the hot tea, Kamar followed Selina and caught up with her before she left The Greenhouse.

What on earth had his father said to cause Selina's intense reaction? Kamar had thought they were getting along brilliantly, better than he had any right to expect, given the unconventional manner in which their marriage had begun. He knew the cliché, that the course of true love never did run smoothly, but he'd hoped that he'd smoothed out all the bumps so the passage to love was now clear.

As the days had passed, he had come to know the depth of Selina's character, the simple pleasure he found in her company, the joy of receiving her love. He had not previously imagined or understood the happiness that could come with commitment to one woman, but he now realized that the commitment provided unexpected rewards.

He had been forced to learn her, to know her completely, and in so doing, had come to love her.

Peter Pan was grounded, and he'd discovered that he liked the earth. Loved it, actually.

But now Selina, like Peter's Wendy, was gone. Not kidnapped by Captain Hook, but worse. She was running away.

He wouldn't let her, but, perhaps sensing he followed, Selina veered off the main path onto a slippery track that led beneath the waterfall. She ducked beneath its sheltering spray, then turned to face him.

"What?" she snapped.

He waved his hands in the air. "We were getting along so well. What did my father say?"

She crossed her arms over her chest. "Enough. Apparently he ordered you to make up with me because you need a steadying influence."

Kamar sighed with exasperation. Why couldn't the old man have been more tactful? "That is true, but—"

"But what?" Her face was streaked with tears, or perhaps the spray from the waterfall had condensed on her reddened, angry cheeks.

"But sometimes my father..." Frustrated, Kamar stopped and shook his head. "He has an uncanny gift for being right for the wrong reasons."

"Oh, really? Forgive me, but your father's idiosyncrasies aren't of interest to me right now. At least he had the backbone to tell me the truth. Why didn't you come clean with me? Why didn't you just tell me why you'd decided you wanted to stay married?"

"Because that wasn't the entire story. And if you'd wished to know, why didn't you ask?"

"I had wondered about your motivation, but you were being so nice to me that I…I didn't question it." She bit her lip. "I was stupid. But no more. Excuse me." She tried to push past him, evidently intending to leave.

"Wait!" He put a hand on her arm. "As I said, my father is often correct, but for the wrong reasons. He wanted us to stay together because it was the right thing to do. I wanted us to stay together because I wanted you."

She sniffed.

"I still do, and I know you want me."

"That's not enough," she said, her voice raw and husky. "That's not enough to carry us through everything that life will throw at us, and we both know it."

"You are right, of course. Listen to me, Selina." He rubbed water out of his face. "I always knew that I'd have to grow up, that I couldn't go on the way I had. With all the women."

"Thanks for letting me know." Her tone was bitter.

"I am approaching my thirtieth year." He took her by the shoulders. "A time of much reflection. I knew I would have to settle down, but could I love?"

"Can you?" She met his eyes, her gaze direct and unafraid.

Her raw, pure courage opened his heart even wider. There was no one on this earth like his Selina. She truly was a goddess. That she loved him was beyond fortunate. Surely he had been blessed.

"Yes," he whispered. "I have discovered in the

last few days, that I indeed know how to love someone with all of myself, body and soul. A very special
woman, one who has survived the travails of life and
grown strong from them. One who I hope will accept
me with all my flaws and faults.''

She stared at him without speaking, her eyes filling
with tears.

His throat thickened, but he managed to force
words out. ''I love you. Will you not be mine? For I
am certain that you love me.''

''Yes,'' she whispered. ''I do. I didn't think that I
could love anyone, but I do. I know that I'd be lost
and miserable without you.''

He grabbed her, there under the waterfall, with the
wild splash and spray all around them. He grabbed
her and squeezed her tight. He'd never let her go.
''Then we'll live together as husband and wife, in that
house in D.C.?''

''Yes, as husband and wife, in the home we'll make
together.'' She laughed, tossing her head back, loving
him, loving everything: the water flowing through her
hair and down her neck; Kam, with his lips on her
throat, her mouth, kissing her exultantly; even adoring
that neediness, that itchy twitchiness that led her to
press her hips against his and murmur into his ear,
''Let's go back to the villa. I have a date with a bed.
And you.''

Epilogue

After registering, Kamar led his family out of the lobby toward the villa they'd rented, with a nanny and a bellman straggling behind with the luggage.

He looked down at the red head of his four-year-old daughter and knew he was tempting fate. He said to Selina, "I wonder if bringing both children was wise. Especially Leila."

Selina chuckled. His wife had grown more beautiful with every passing day, and he loved her more and more as he uncovered the depths of her soul. Today she wore loose white linen, as he did, with her red-gold hair high in a twist, so that neither of their little ones could tug at the strands. Behind her meandered Leila's nanny, a young woman in imminent danger of losing all her marbles—she just didn't know it yet.

Kamar thought of her as Number Nine, or was she Ms. Eight? At this point the names of Leila's long-suffering nannies eluded him. He simply couldn't keep up.

"I'm sure there will be plenty of activities for Leila," Selina said. "She'll be fine."

The object of their scrutiny toddled between them, dressed in a pink-and-white sailor-style pinafore. She tilted her head and smiled at him. "I love you, baba-Daddy." She slipped her little, soft hand confidingly into his.

He narrowed his eyes at her, knowing full well that behind her angelic gaze dwelt the soul of an imp. As inventive as she was mischievous, Leila wreaked chaos wherever she went. Selina called their daughter "creative." Kamar preferred "demonic."

In her short life, Leila had caused the resignations of no fewer than eight nannies. Among her transgressions, his daughter liked to slide down the embassy banisters attired only in her underwear. She had decorated the entry hall of their home with crayoned murals, complete with palm trees and brownish blobs she claimed were camels. She'd signed her work with large black letters in both Arabic and English. When confronted, she'd explained that she'd drawn pictures on the walls "like in Gwandpa's palace." In fairness, the palace in Zohra-zbel did indeed have mosaic murals on many walls. Though they'd had to remove her art, her drawing and writing were remarkably good for a four-year-old, Kamar thought.

Although he adored her, he'd been afraid that Leila would be jealous of her baby brother, Prince Kahlil, who now napped serenely in the stroller Selina pushed. On the contrary, Kahlil stood in danger of being killed by Leila's kindness. She did not seem to grasp that the baby couldn't be her best friend, and that Kahlil was too young to slide down the banisters with her or ride on the dog's broad back as though their golden retriever was a pony. She didn't understand the concept of "later."

In that she was her father's daughter. He also believed that ultimately the moment was all that existed.

And at this moment he was nervous. Very nervous. The only time he could recall being more edgy was at this place, when he was desperately wooing Selina.

"We should have brought another servant," he said to Selina. "Perhaps the cook."

She lifted her brows, and he could practically read her mind. *Arrogant.* She said, "We don't need a retinue. Besides, I remember that you cooked for me here quite well."

"That was such a crazy situation."

She skirted the edge of the Oasis pool. "Well, we dined out on that story for years. I thought it excellent party conversation."

Kamar snorted. "It was maddening."

"Oh, we've been through worse."

"When?"

"How about the time when Leila decided that the Syrian ambassador's son needed a haircut?"

They laughed, and Leila giggled. He glanced at his daughter. "We shouldn't encourage her. Fortunately, you smoothed over the situation nicely." Kamar blessed the day he'd persuaded his wife to abandon her PR job to work by his side. Before her, he'd struggled, but Selina's excellent organizational skills had made her essential. He couldn't do without her.

"Leila's going to give some unfortunate man fits one day," she said.

"She is giving a man fits right now."

Selina smiled. "The blessing is that they're different. Leila is playful and Kahlil, calm."

They'd reached the villa, and after the bellman opened the door, stepped inside.

"Where am I sleeping, baba?" Leila demanded.

"Down here," Kamar said. They'd rented a three-bedroom villa, with two bedrooms downstairs and a spacious master suite on the upper level. The baby would sleep in the nanny's room; Leila, who was a restless sleeper, would have her own room; he and Selina would get some peace and private time upstairs.

At least that was the idea. Kamar assumed that at 5:30 a.m. Leila would wake up, steal the baby out of his crib, and bring him upstairs for a nap with Mommy and Daddy. His heart warmed at the thought. Despite the early hour, cuddling with his family was the greatest delight he'd ever known. And he enjoyed it every day.

He had never anticipated such happiness in his life, and it had all started here, in this place, most unexpectedly, with the phony engagement to Selina. His wife had turned out to be so much more than he'd guessed. The mouthy American girl had become the love of his life.

She brought out the best in him, and he was grateful.

He was a very lucky fellow.

The next morning Selina awakened with her head tucked into her husband's shoulder and her daughter's high-pitched voice coming from downstairs.

"Don't dwop it, Kahlil."

Oh, *ixzit*. What was she doing now? Don't drop what? Selina blinked, becoming aware of the gray dawn light filtering through the thin sheers at the window and the red digital clock near her reading seven-thirty.

"Two extra hours," she mumbled. "I suppose I should be grateful."

"What?" Kam stirred, and she stroked his chest.

"Nothing," she whispered, loving him. "Go back to sleep. I'll take care of it." Her husband worked his tail off, what with controversy after controversy plaguing the Middle East.

Now his eyes popped open. "Take care of what?"

She sat up. "Whatever's going on downstairs." Now she could hear the rattle of china and spoons on a tray.

"*Ixzit*," he said. "Leila has fixed us breakfast."

"*Ixzit* is right. She can't possibly bring it upstairs, not with Kahlil."

"We'll have to punish her. Didn't we forbid her to go into the kitchen alone?"

"We can't start off the vacation that way," Selina said. She could hear a succession of irregular thumps as the children struggled upstairs. Then she heard the nanny's voice.

"Oh, that's all right." Kam, evidently also having heard the nanny, settled back against the pillows.

"We'd better put some clothes on." She got out of bed and went to the closet.

"This place used to supply robes," Kam said.

She reached inside the closet and took out two terry cloth robes. "They still do, very nice ones."

Dressed, they waited until the children and their nanny trailed into the room in a three-person parade. Kahlil led the way, crawling with a determined look on his face and a spoon clutched in one chubby hand. Leila followed with empty mugs, and the nanny staggered under the weight of a loaded tea tray. Kam leaped up to grab it from her. He set it down on a little table in the corner of the room and started to help the nanny serve morning tea.

"I'm sorry," the nanny said. "She woke me up and insisted. I remembered that you usually get up at five-thirty, so..." She shrugged and started to pour.

"It's just fine, Alice." Selina hoped she sounded soothing. She wanted to keep this nanny around for a few more weeks. Alice had already lasted five months; six was the average tenure of one of Leila's nannies. Selina prayed that this vacation wouldn't drive Alice screaming into the Gulf or back to D.C. La Torchere had numerous opportunities for Leila's creativity to express itself. Selina had a brief vision of her daughter climbing to the top of The Greenhouse waterfall with Kahlil in tow, and shuddered.

"What is it, Sellie?" Kam touched her hand.

"Nothing. Let's keep an eye on Leila while we're here, all right?"

"Of course. You know, we could buy her a leash." He grinned.

She frowned. "That isn't funny."

"I wanna leash! I wanna leash!" Leila sang.

"You do not," Selina said. "You don't know what a leash is."

"Yes I do. Like Tallie has," Leila referred to the dog.

"Yes, just like Tallie." Kam sipped tea.

"Why din't we bwing Tallie?" Leila asked.

"He stayed home to keep Grandpa Jerry company," Selina said.

"Oh, yeah." Leila examined her mug with a discontented expression, then reached for the sugar bowl.

When everyone was settled with mugs of warm, sweet tea, and the nanny had tactfully left, Selina looked around the room at three happy faces.

Leila chattered, dumped more sugar into her tea and drank, spilling it down the front of her nightgown. Kam held Kahlil on his lap, bouncing him up and down. They sang about the itsy bitsy spider while the baby banged his spoon on the table.

Her heart swelled, and she found herself blinking away tears.

She could barely remember her past, before Kam had brought joy into her life. Without Kam, her world had been like an endless, cloudy day, with no sunshine to relieve the dull gloom. Her existence had been all surface and no substance, like a cheap snack of cotton candy and popcorn. Loving, rich and varied, her marriage was a feast. Every bright new day brought fresh experiences and unexpected delights.

Selina had never been happier.

* * * * *

IN A FAIRY TALE WORLD...

*Six reluctant couples. Five classic love
stories. One matchmaking princess.
And time is running out!*

*Don't miss the continuation of
this magical miniseries.*

*NIGHTTIME SWEETHEARTS
by Cara Colter
Silhouette Romance 1754
Available February 2005*

*TWICE A PRINCESS
by Susan Meier
Silhouette Romance 1758
Available March 2005*

SILHOUETTE *Romance*®

Discover the enchanting power of love in

KISSED BY CAT
Silhouette Romance #1757

by **Shirley Jump**

Cursed by an evil witch unless she fell in love in six days, Catherine Wyndham's life would drastically change. She believed it was impossible—until she accepted a job with Garrett McAllister, a sexy vet with dark secrets of his own....

Soulmates

Some things are meant to be...

On sale February 2005!
Only from Silhouette Books!

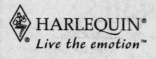

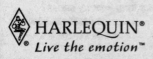

COMING NEXT MONTH

#1754 NIGHTTIME SWEETHEARTS—Cara Colter
In a Fairy Tale World...

She never forgot the brooding bad boy who had, once upon a time, made her heart race. So when Cynthia Fosythe hears a husky, familiar voice calling to her out of the tropical moonlit night she's stunned. She'd let go of Rick Barnett to preserve her good-girl image, but now Cynthia's prepared to lay it all on the line for another chance at paradise.

#1755 INSTANT MARRIAGE, JUST ADD GROOM—Myrna Mackenzie

Nortorious bachelor Caleb Fremont is just what baby-hungry Victoria Holbrook is looking for—the perfect candidate for the father of her child. Although Caleb isn't interested in being a dad, he's agreed to a temporary marriage of convenience. But when the stick finally turns pink will he be able to let Victoria—and his baby—go?

#1756 DADDY, HE WROTE—Jill Limber

Reclusive author Ian Miller purchased an historic farmhouse to get some much-needed peace and quiet—and overcome his writer's block. Yet when he finds that the farm comes complete with beautiful caretaker Trish Ryan and her delightful daughter, Ian might find that inspiration can be found in the most unlikely places....

#1757 KISSED BY CAT—Shirley Jump
Soulmates

When Garrett McCallister discovers a purr-fectly gorgeous woman in his veterinary clinic, wearing nothing but a lab coat, he's confused, suspicious...and very imtrigued. Will Garrett run when he discovers Catherine Wyndham's secret curse, or will he let the mysterious siren into his heart?

SRCNM0105

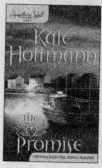
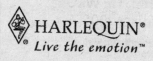
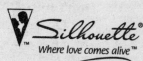